Eat, Drink, and Be Wary

A Sleuth Sisters Mystery

By Maggie Pill

Gwendolyn Press, Michigan, USA

Eat, Drink, and Be Wary/Maggie Pill — 1st ed.
SBN: 978-1-944502-10-2

This one's for Gina, with thanks for her expert advice.

Chapter One

Retta

My pitch for the Smart Detective Agency's next case was going well until Barbara Ann went all women's lib on me. We sat in her office, Barbara behind the desk, sipping her special-blend coffee, mailed each month from Seattle. Faye and I sat next to each other in comfortable but kind of plain blue-upholstered chairs. Faye held a glass of iced tea in one hand while she jotted down notes with the other. I had a smoothie I'd bought on the way over at a little shop open only in the summer months, when northern Michigan actually has people in it.

"The FBI wants the Smart Detective Agency to go undercover for them." My palms warmed as I came to the sticky spot, and I cupped my drink to cool them. "We'd attend a Love-Able Ladies Retreat at an inn near Traverse City."

I was hoping that *undercover* and *FBI* would overshadow *Love-Able Ladies*, but Barbara gasped in outrage. I went on quickly, before she could start in.

"It's this weekend, August 12th to the 14th, at the St. Millicent Winery on the Leelanau Peninsula."

Known for geographic beauty and classy events, the area north of Traverse City is a place a person doesn't have to be a wine lover to enjoy. St. Millicent's was the newest winery/inn on the Leelanau, and according to what I'd read, it had lovely views of Grand Traverse Bay, plush accommodations, notable wines, and meals to die for. If I convinced my sisters to take the case, we'd get to experience it for ourselves.

"What would our job be?" Faye's voice betrayed doubt, since she generally prefers staying close to home. I was confident I could convince Faye to go along once I dealt with Barbara's objections.

"We're supposed to get acquainted with a fashion designer who's introducing her new line of clothing at the retreat. Her father's suspected of being a big-time criminal, and the FBI hopes she might help them stop him."

It was a perfect case for us. The only obstacle was Barbara Ann.

My oldest sister wasn't distracted by talk of the FBI. "I've heard of the Love-Able Ladies." Her voice turned sarcastically girlish. "'If you want a better man, be a better woman.' Seriously, Retta?"

That was the bump in my road. Love-Able Ladies was sort of a traveling celebration of femininity, encouraging "old-fashioned girls" to cultivate modesty and acknowledge that their place in society was a few steps behind their fathers, husbands, and sons. The organizers held retreats at various elegant resorts around the nation and railed against "bullying feminism." The attendees were mostly well-to-do women who didn't work outside the home and didn't want to. The tone of their gatherings was self-congratulatory and a little self-righteous, with a lot of talk about "the civilizing influence" of wives and mothers.

It wasn't the type of thing Barbara went for. Not at all.

Because I wanted to see St. Millicent's, and because I don't mind being called a *girl* at fifty-plus, I was determined we'd take the FBI up on their offer. "So they're a little over the top on the pleasing men thing," I argued. "We don't have to agree with them to enjoy a weekend of fine wine and beautiful scenery."

"*I* refuse to even *listen* to that garbage." Barbara used her I'm-not-kidding voice. "Women died for the right to stand next to men in this world, Retta. *Those* women would drag us all back to the days of barefoot and pregnant."

Looking at the flyer I'd downloaded and brought along, Faye commented, "Apparently not barefoot. One of the sponsors is Bellarina Shoes—at three hundred dollars a pair."

"Another sickening thing." Barbara was getting wound up. "They get a bunch of trophy wives together then present them with tables full of items they don't need at ridiculous prices."

"Hey, it's no secret that girls love to shop."

Without moving a muscle, Barbara climbed up on her high horse. "We aren't *girls*, Retta, and neither *all* men nor *all* women love *any*thing. You might spend hours picking out this week's nail design, but I certainly do not."

I could have pointed out how much nicer her nails would look coated in a tangerine shade to match her blouse, but I'm not that dumb. Faye curled her own fingers out of sight, establishing a neutral position.

Barbara Ann is what used to be called a bluestocking: intelligent, well-educated, and a little dowdy, though I don't think that last one is a bluestocking requirement. Her clothing runs to navy and black; her favorite jewelry is a gold chain she's had for years along with two basic wristwatches, one silver, one gold. She wears almost no makeup, just light blush and a moisturizing lipstick that hardly shows.

Because I'd anticipated her reaction, I had my arguments ready. "This is a chance to enhance the reputation of our firm." The Smart Detective Agency had done some good things in its first few years, but there were still lots of people who thought three middle-aged women running a business like ours was a joke.

My remark hit home since Barbara really wants respect for the agency, but she wasn't quite ready to agree with me. "I don't see how going anywhere near the Love-Able Ladies gains us respect."

"If you don't like the assignment, Barbara, you could stay home."

She practically vibrated with shock, and though I kept my expression innocent, I smiled to myself. Which would my sister give up: her feminist principles or control of a case? Delaying the decision, she asked, "Why doesn't the FBI use its own agents?"

"Love-Able Ladies events are age-specific. There are retreats for women under thirty and some for thirty to fifty. This one is for fifty and over." When Barbara's brow rose I added, "The rationale is that attendees are more comfortable with others of the same age."

"I get that." Faye is the middle child and therefore less judgmental (bossy) than our eldest. "There'd be some comfort in knowing you're in a group where everyone is dealing with a fifty-plus, saggy body."

Grateful for her support, I forged on. "They also like that we really live in northern Michigan. It adds to our credibility."

"And being private detectives isn't a problem?" Barbara tried not to sound sarcastic, but she does, just a little, all the time.

"We won't mention that. Just a housewife and a widow." That was a mistake, because Barbara realized I'd already left her out of my scenario. I hurried on. "Faye and I could be convincing, but—" I met Barbara's gaze, leaving the rest of the statement for her to finish. If anyone stuck out at a retreat like this one, it would be a woman who'd spent her life working alongside men in the tough hallways of justice. Barbara had never been anyone's wife, trophy or otherwise.

Looking right back at me, she repeated her question. "Why us?"

"Agent Auburn heard about me from Lars. He thinks I can connect with Dina Engel, the crime boss' daughter, because of the fashion thing. You know I love that."

"And the assignment would be what again?"

"I meet this Dina and build rapport with her. If at some point in the weekend she seems receptive, I mention that my boyfriend is with the FBI and can protect witnesses who testify against criminal relatives. I give her my phone number, and she leaves the retreat with a way to contact the Bureau if she's sick of living with a drug lord."

"Why do they think she might be amenable to such an approach at this point in time?"

Barbara always talks like that.

"The agent who contacted me, Chet Auburn, says Roger Engel was horrible to his wife," I replied. "Sleazy affairs with women from his night clubs, that kind of thing. He wasn't much of a father either."

"He's got just the one daughter?"

"Dina. She was married once, but her husband died in a car crash. In 2010 her mother got really sick with diabetes, and she moved home to take care of her. After Mrs. Engel died, Dina apparently decided she wanted to have a career."

"In clothing design."

"Right. Engel was against it at first, but she stood up to him. With her mother's death and her insistence on doing something of her own, Auburn thinks Dina's had a change of attitude that might benefit the Bureau."

"She's been a criminal's kid her whole life and now she's going to turn on her only remaining relative?"

I shrugged. "If it doesn't work, they'll try something else."

Barbara tapped her pen on the desk pad for a few seconds. "Fashion talk, Love-Able Ladies—it's not me."

I felt a little thrill at how easy that had been. "Which is exactly why Faye and I should go." I kept my voice casual, as if the two of us handled cases without Barbara Ann all the time. Faye wore an expression of mild terror at the thought of going somewhere and meeting strangers without Barbara to guide her, but I'd deal with that later. "Someone should mind the office, and as you say, this isn't your cup of tea, or glass of wine, in this case."

Barbara knew she was being herded toward a decision, but she wasn't sure how to change direction. "How dangerous is this case you volunteered us for likely to be?"

I rolled my eyes. "I didn't volunteer. Agent Auburn called me."

"Have you met the man?"

"No, but he and Lars worked together in New Mexico." I raised my palms in a question. "Would my boyfriend ask me to do something dangerous?"

Barbara had to shake her head. Lars Johannsen had helped us out with a couple of cases now, and we all trusted him. Still, she was reluctant. "Going anywhere near this woman seems like trouble to me."

"*If* Ms. Engel is willing to talk about her father, we offer her a way to contact the FBI. If not, we give Auburn our impressions so he can decide what she might respond to in the future."

"Like what?"

I ticked off examples on my fingers. "Emotional appeal, financial reward, guarantee of immunity, or assurance of protection."

Faye's expression became concerned. "Is she afraid of her father?"

"If she isn't, she should be. Bad things happen to people who cross Roger Engel." That was bound to get Faye on my side. Her soft heart demands that she help those who are mistreated in any way. But the argument was a two-edged sword. While Faye made a sound of sympathy for poor Dina Engel, Barbara practically pounced on my admission. "Then this job could be dangerous."

"Engel won't be anywhere near Traverse City." I went over it again. "We chat Dina up and take it as far as we can. That's it." I looked to Faye for support.

"It sounds like something Retta would be good at," she said, and I let out a little sigh. Faye was on my side. That was half the battle, but if we had to drag Barbara along, her twitchy left eyebrow would betray how much she disapproved of everything Love-Able. We were much better off if she stayed home.

To my surprise and delight, Barbara agreed. "I vote we help the Bureau with their case, but you two attend the retreat without me."

I didn't look at Faye, who was no doubt equally amazed and afraid. Me? I was thrilled. The two younger sisters had a case all our own. That's what I call an opportunity for growth.

Chapter Two

Faye

While Retta confirmed the details of our weekend and Barb went off to finish our only current case, I researched Dina Engel. There wasn't much about her online until the last six months, when a website featuring her upcoming line of clothing had appeared. "Detroit Chic" had an official launch date in September, but on the last morning of the Love-Able Ladies retreat she planned to do a "mini-reveal" as a way of building buzz. Though they weren't yet available for sale, getting a hundred well-heeled Michigan women interested in her designs was a nice initial step.

While there was plenty of information about Detroit Chic on the internet, there was little about the company's designer/owner. The About Us section on the website had a few pictures of Dina at work, but in most she had her back to the camera. There were articles in the *Detroit Free Press* about how great her enterprise might be for the city, but there was almost nothing about Dina herself. The only clear picture revealed a petite woman of perhaps forty with soft blond hair. She looked slightly Slavic, with a round face that had begun to show both age and incipient weight. In the picture she wore ragged low-rise jeans, a shirt with epaulettes, and those flat tennis shoe throwbacks that made my feet hurt just looking at them. Either Dina spent a lot of time sitting or she was able to tolerate a lot more pain than I could.

The Smart Detective Agency had "special" connections, meaning paid sites that let us snoop into peoples' lives. There wasn't much to find about Dina, no credit cards or credit history, but two things did catch my interest. First she'd received a bachelor's degree in fashion design back in 2000, so Detroit Chic was probably the resurgence of an old dream. Second, an item in the *Detroit News* mentioned her marriage to attorney Daryl Sweet in 2008. Sweet's death in a car accident was reported two years later, and Dina had apparently taken back her maiden name afterward. That was all I could find: statistics and dry facts. Nothing personal, nothing scandalous, nothing humanitarian. It seemed the woman's life had been spent outside the limelight: protected daughter, invisible wife, silent widow, and if Retta's information was correct, for the last few years, her mother's main caregiver.

What kind of person was she? The FBI thought her mother's death had changed Dina, and I understood that. There's nothing like the passing of the previous generation to remind us that life is fleeting. Had Mom's death made the daughter determined to make something of her life? Had she stepped out of Papa's control? Or didn't she care where the family money came from as long as she got what she wanted?

Next I looked up Dina's father, Roger Engel. The son of Swedish immigrants and originally named Rutgar Engla, he showed up in police data bases many times in his youth. Only one arrest stuck, a two-year sentence for car theft at nineteen. The experience apparently help the kid wise up, because after that he'd hired better lawyers and beaten every attempt to lay a crime at his door. He was, as Retta mentioned, known for licentious living and multiple affairs, the typical "Look what I can get!" mentality of a man who hasn't got a clue what being a man is about. Looking at an array of photos taken over the years, I saw that old Roger had paid for his fast-paced lifestyle by aging badly. The smirking, Viking-like youth in his long-ago mug shot was now a bloated toad who looked ready for a visit from the Grim Reaper.

I was still reading about Engel's alleged criminal activities when Retta stowed her phone in her gym-bag-sized purse and announced that our weekend at the retreat was arranged. "It was fully booked, but Auburn made two registered attendees an offer they couldn't refuse."

"What?"

She giggled. "Not like in *The Godfather,* silly. They 'won' a trip to Cancun that has to be taken next weekend. Your name and mine magically appeared in their spots."

Since Barb wasn't around, I said, "Tell me about Love-Able Ladies. I've heard it mentioned, but I don't know a lot."

She'd done her homework. "Love-Able Ladies was started by a woman named Angel Sonoma—and if you believe that's her real name, I'll sell you my shares in the Mackinac Bridge." She stopped abruptly and shook her empty smoothie cup. "I don't suppose you have any iced tea."

It was a joke, because I always have iced tea. Without a word I rose and led the way to the kitchen, where she sat down at our three-person table and I headed for the fridge. "Angel Sonoma claims women were happier when they accepted their roles as wives and mothers and tried to be good examples of virtue and respectability."

"I guess that's okay for people who don't have to earn a living."

She took a sip of the tea I set before her. "Here's what Barbara hates. According to their philosophy, women should try to be appealing to men and never, ever compete with them. Societies are stronger when males take the lead and females content themselves with hearth, home, and being beautiful."

"Like when we used to get traded for cattle." While I wasn't as upset by the whole anti-feminist thing as Barb was, I recognized the unfairness of letting one sex judge the other's value.

"It boils down to self-confidence," Retta argued. "If men respond positively to a woman, her ego gets a little boost, and maybe she's worth a few more cows."

I shook my head. "And to make them respond positively, we have to dress in uncomfortable clothes, hide our faces with makeup, and pretend we don't understand compound interest?"

Her tone turned irritated. "I'm not arguing their case, Faye. You asked what Loveable Ladies is about. It's a lot about women wanting to be women."

Though Barb would have had a dozen counterarguments, I'm not a fan of philosophical debate. I sat down with my own refilled glass of tea and listened as Retta went on about "our" weekend plan.

As she spoke, I began having doubts about three days of elbow-rubbing with a hundred Love-Able Ladies. I wouldn't fit in, and besides, I'm uncomfortable in large groups of strangers. While I agreed that Barb's contempt, which she couldn't and wouldn't hide, would stand in the way of our goal, the thought of going without her made me nervous. Retta rattled on though, and I knew my discomfort wasn't going to change anything. Despite my misgivings, two sister detectives would soon visit the Leelanau Peninsula.

Chapter Three

Barb

Retta thought she'd been clever about convincing me to opt out of the retreat, but I'd known her far too long to be taken in. She wanted this case for her own, and she was taking Faye along because she can boss her around. As the baby of the family, Retta's used to getting her way, but at times I step in, purely for her own good. Nobody should get what she wants with just a smile and a few bats of her glued-on eyelashes.

I've read the theories about family placement and personality, and they're as true as a lot of other memes out there. Retta is the classic youngest child, a charming entertainer. Being oldest, I like things done correctly, and Faye is a typical middler, with a relaxed view of life (other than a fear of bridges and formal gatherings) and a weak view of her own importance.

Retta was our parents' changeling, too cosmopolitan for a farm couple from the rural environs of a small town. From early on she was too smooth for two people who never imagined they'd create something so beautiful and sparkly. Though Mom and Dad tried, Retta was always a law unto herself. When Faye and I started our detective agency, we'd meant to leave her out, but it was like trying to keep a puppy out of your living room. If you're there, that's where the puppy wants to be.

Remaining in Allport didn't mean I was staying out of the new case. I'd noted the name of the agent who contacted Retta, and after I delivered a final report to our latest client, I called the Detroit FBI office and asked to speak with Agent Chester Auburn.

He was cautious until I explained who I was and gave him time to confirm it. I told him a little about my background as an assistant district attorney in Seattle and my concern that my sisters might be unwittingly putting themselves into danger by agreeing to help with his case. Once he was convinced I wasn't simply being nosy, Auburn took my request for information seriously.

"I worked in Albuquerque until recently," he told me. "I knew Lars Johannsen had female friends in northern Michigan who were P.I.s, so with the short timeline I've got on this project, I thought I'd see if you were interested."

"You're after Roger Engel."

He paused, apparently considering how honest to be. "When I transferred to Detroit a few months back, one of my first tasks was questioning him about a woman who was murdered just after she called us and said she wanted to talk."

"About Engel?"

"That's what we think, but we never heard what she had to say. She was killed in an apparent drive-by shooting that same night. Now there are enough of those that it might have been a coincidence, but it happens a lot."

"When Engel's organization is threatened, people die." I'd seen enough of that in Washington to know that life is cheap for the worst of society's criminals.

"The guy's arrogant but he's good, and his people jump when he says jump."

"So you need a way to get to him."

"Right. When I read about Detroit Chic in the paper, I started thinking maybe the daughter would help. He's not much of a father and never has been, though she never wanted for anything money can buy."

"Where does it come from?"

"Mostly drugs, but as a former ADA you know there are plenty of other crimes that go along with that. His legitimate business—if you want to call it that—is running several 'gentlemen's clubs.' On the illegitimate side, he's probably Michigan's biggest importer of opium."

Having worked on the Pacific coast, I knew a little about smuggling. "How does he bring it in?"

Fabric rustled, and I imagined Auburn shrugging. "The methods change. We stop a pipeline; he builds another one. We've seen the stuff come in by water, air, even by train from Canada."

"I've seen how creative they can be: South American drugs hidden in sacks of coffee, Asian drugs inside toys and soldiers' keepsakes."

"Creative, yeah." He cleared his throat. "That's why it would be great to enlist the help of someone inside Engel's organization. If we had prior information, we might catch him with the goods."

"And you think that someone could be the daughter."

"She's been in the background her whole life. Now she's spreading her wings, as they say."

"But Daddy's helping her." I tried to imagine Engels' motivation. Was he trying to win his daughter's love at this late date? Was he an aging criminal who regretted his sins? Taking a different tack, I wondered if he was a savvy businessman who planned to use his daughter's new enterprise to launder dirty money.

I'd sort through that later. "If Dina is starting a business with her father's money, why would she help the Bureau take him down?"

"Engel's no philanthropist. Word is he gave Dina a strict budget and two years to make the business a success. But if he went to jail—" He left the rest to my imagination.

"She'd get his money, at least some of it."

"Right. Whatever the government lets her keep as a reward for her help." Auburn cleared his throat. "Honestly, Ms. Evans, we don't know enough about Dina Engel to say what she might be willing to do. There's a good chance she dislikes her father."

"And you're hoping she's reached a break-away point."

He made a sound that indicated hopefulness. "Lots of people hit an age where they want a chance at the life they never got."

"Like starting a detective agency at fifty-something?"

Auburn chuckled. "I guess." He made his own confession. "Last year at forty-five, I parachuted out of a plane, I think to prove to myself I could still do what I did back in jump school."

"Your choice was far more logical than mine." I shifted in my chair. "Agent Auburn, my sisters don't think I'd do well with the Love-Able Ladies, and I have to agree with them. They're going without me."

"I take it you aren't the type to jump when a man says jump."

"Not now, not ever. Still, I need to know my sisters aren't taking on something that could land them in trouble."

He did me the courtesy of thinking about it. "I can't see any way this could endanger them. We just want their impression of Ms. Engel."

"Her daddy isn't going to show up to look over her shoulder?"

"He seems to be hands off on the fashion thing. He gave her the start she wanted. If Dina fails, he let her try. If she succeeds, he looks like the good guy. What's he got to lose?"

"That's true."

Auburn gave me his cell phone number so I could reach him directly, and I added it to my contacts list. "I'll be up there on Friday, so I can help if your sisters need anything," he assured. "All they have to do is eat nice food, drink good wine, listen politely, and smile a lot."

"Faye is a really good listener," I replied, "and the other one can smile her way out of just about anything. I guess you're good to go."

Chapter Four

Retta

Once we'd taken the case, I had to make sure Faye didn't embarrass herself with her clothing choices. My sister is the sweetest, kindest person you'll ever meet, but looks simply don't matter to her. Though she seemed a little annoyed when I made her show me what she planned to take along, it was a good thing I did.

"Faye, the flowers on that shirt are the size of volleyballs."

"It's summertime," she replied. "People wear flowery stuff."

"Skinny Hawaiian people, maybe. You want solid-colored shirts with big jewelry."

"Do I?" Her tone was a warning.

"Faye, I'm just trying to help." I peered into her closet. "Maybe we could look online."

She frowned. "I hate online shopping. Nothing ever fits, and I have to send it back."

I glanced at the calendar. "We don't have a lot of time, either. Tomorrow we'll see what they have at Marian's."

"She charges an arm and a leg for everything," Faye objected. "I'll look at—"

"Don't say it!" I warned. "You are *not* buying clothing for this weekend at a store where you also buy your groceries."

Her expression turned what Mom would have called bull-headed. "I do it all the time."

Barbara leaned against the door frame, smirking. There was no sense appealing to her for help, because A) she isn't great at fashion herself, and B) she thinks anything Faye does is all right. Happily, she got bored after a few minutes and went back to her precious computer.

Ignoring Faye's "But it's comfortable" excuses, I kept sliding hangers down the closet rod. In the end I found a couple of decent tops, one I'd bought her for her birthday (probably never worn) and one with a decent cut and a designer name (no doubt from a resale shop). At the back of the closet I found the dress she'd bought for my daughter's wedding ten years ago. Cut in a timeless style that draped nicely and emphasized Faye's height rather than her girth, I decided with updated accessories it would work for the formal dinner on Saturday evening.

"You need one more outfit," I told her. "Tomorrow we'll see what Marian has on clearance." I glanced at the small box on her dresser. "I have enough jewelry for both of us."

"You have enough jewelry for a revival of *Hello, Dolly*," Faye said, but her comment seemed more resigned than angry. After a moment she said, "Maybe you should take Barb with you."

I glanced at the empty doorway. "You know she'd be a disaster."

"Okay, then I could go but stay in the room, in case you need me."

Faye was starting to feel antsy, as she does when she has to meet more than one stranger at a time. "We're both going to this retreat, and we're going to have a ball," I told her. "I'll be with you all the time, and you're going to feel like a fairy tale princess."

Looking up from where she'd knelt to dig her "good" underwear out of a bottom drawer, she grinned. "Does that mean I have to sleep for a hundred years or be shut up in a castle guarded by a dragon?"

"Neither," I responded. "We're the kind of princesses who solve our own problems, with or without dragons."

Chapter Five

Faye

When I told Dale about the case and the Love-Able Ladies Retreat, he expressed surprise that I'd attend a "girly" event. He grinned when he said it, but I couldn't smile back. I was having major second thoughts.

"I won't fit in." I set a grilled cheese sandwich in front of him, perfectly done if I do say it myself. "You know I'm not good in groups."

Dale's eyes met mine. "How many groups have you been part of in the last decade?"

"Church is about it," I confessed. Moving to the sink, I set a colander of vegetables I'd brought home from our sons' farm on the edge to drain. Sitting, I took a bite of my own sandwich.

"Don't decide how it's going to be beforehand," Dale advised. "It might be fun."

"Hanging with a bunch of women who are all about looks and acting lady-like?"

"You look good, and you're some lady in my book."

I felt my eyes widen, but he dipped his sandwich in his tomato soup and took another bite, as if he'd said something totally normal. When I kept staring, he shrugged. "What?"

"Dale, I'm thirty pounds overweight. I have wrinkles around my mouth from years of smoking. My hair is graying fast, and I battle constantly to keep my two eyebrows from becoming one."

"And what's wrong with that?"

I shook my head. "Do you call that looking good?"

He smiled. "I do."

"Then you're seeing me through the eyes of love."

Dale raised his hands, palms up. "Is there another way to see your wife of thirty-odd years?"

After I'd hugged my husband of thirty-four years (He can never remember the exact number) and sent him back outside, Buddy and I went for a walk. My dog needed the exercise and so did I, but I also had to talk myself back into attending the retreat. I couldn't let Retta go alone, and Barb simply didn't have the self-restraint to be her backup. She'd be arguing women's rights with some Love-Able Lady within fifteen minutes of arrival.

You can do this, I told myself. *All you have to do is follow Retta around and smile a lot.*

But they would all be judging me. I've never liked being held to strangers' unknown—but somehow discernable—standards.

Buddy growled, and I looked up to see a couple of teenagers approaching. Abused before we met, my dog doesn't like strangers much—or people in general, for that matter. "Behave, Bud," I told him, and he let them pass without further comment. While he feels compelled to show his tough side, Buddy trusts me to make the judgment calls.

One hundred fashion-centered, appearance-obsessed women. Women who'd ask each other why I let myself go—why I didn't do something with my hair and how I missed the memo on tooth-whitening gels. They'd look at Retta and wonder how she ended up with a sister like me.

Let me spend my time with animals or one-on-one with people who already like me. Then I'm okay, even pretty good lots of times.

As Buddy watered Mr. Winans' lilac bush, I told myself to stop being a baby. We had a case that required schmoozing, and I'd cope somehow. Still, I vowed to stick close to Retta the whole time on this one. I didn't want to have to cope alone.

Chapter Six

Barb

With nothing pressing at the agency, I spent the afternoon researching Roger Engel. There was a lot of innuendo and not much substance in news reports. Engel was infamous, as Auburn had indicated, but nobody seemed able to give specifics. He ran a string of night clubs, some respectable, most not. When he appeared in public he was always surrounded with guys who looked like extras from a Coppola film.

An anonymous blogger gave what claimed to be an unofficial biography, calling Engel one of Detroit's most successful career criminals.

> *Roger Engel was born on August 12, 1955, the son of Norwegian immigrants living in Clinton Township, Michigan. His father left soon after, abandoning his wife and four children. Engel grew up a charming but out-of-control child. Teachers and neighbors liked him, but he was often in trouble, first at school and later with local police. When his petty crimes turned to more serious ones, he went to prison in 1974.*
>
> *Upon his release, Engel claimed he'd learned his lesson, but if he did, it wasn't the lesson the system intended. Over the next ten years he built a criminal empire in Detroit and surrounding areas, dabbling in several enterprises before reputedly settling on the drug trade.*

Several paragraphs followed on the history of police attempts to document Engel's drug empire, but I skimmed them and focused again when family came up.

Roger married Denise Bishop in 1977. Their relationship lasted almost four decades, though Roger never hid his frequent affairs, mostly with dancers at his clubs. The couple had one child, Dina, born in 1978. In 2008 Dina married Charles Magnum, who she met when he became one of her father's many attorneys. Charles died in a fiery car crash in 2010. They had no children.

I suppressed a desire to comment on the writer's grammar. It should have been "whom she met," but I try not to mix detective business with my efforts to encourage better writing.

There was a recent addendum to the entry.

In early 2016, Dina Engel stepped into the public eye, announcing she would start a clothing design business. Though some dismiss her firm, Detroit Chic, as a rich man's indulgence of his daughter's dreams, Dina claims her work will appeal to women who want to dress stylishly but can't wear the skeleton-sized, body-revealing clothing most designers create. Only time will tell if Ms. Engel has what it takes to succeed in the difficult world of fashion.

I took a look at the Detroit Chic website, which contained preliminary drawings of what Dina planned to offer. I'm not as style clueless as Retta thinks, and I appreciate well-made clothing—just not the youth-chasing, attention-grabbing stuff she often buys. Dina's designs took into account that most women over thirty have things to hide. There wasn't a lot of skin showing, and the clothing flattered the female frame while making allowances for natural maturation. I made note of a few things I might purchase when the line became available. I wouldn't tell Retta, because she'd feel compelled to point out that the dress was black and the pants the darkest navy.

Chapter Seven

Retta

From Tuesday to Thursday, I stayed busy with what I needed to get done before we left Allport. Of course I bought some things for the retreat. Nothing makes a person feel ready for an event like new clothing, shoes, and jewelry. I also made appointments to get my nails done—all twenty of them—and my hair touched up.

Next on the list was seeing to my dog's needs. I decided to ask my nearest neighbors, summer residents who have their own Newfoundland, if Styx could stay with them. Roxie, a spayed female, loves Styx every bit as much as he loves her. I knew they wouldn't say no, even though Styx did have a little accident on their car seat the last time he visited. He gets excited.

My fur baby likes almost everybody, but his positive attitude is sometimes a problem at Faye's. Her dog, Buddy, is about as negative as a dog ever gets, and Styx often has his feelings hurt when we go there. I knew Dale would look out for Styx, but as long as the Coulston family didn't mind, their place was the better choice for a three-day stay. Their son Eli was a cross-country runner, so Styx would get lots of exercise, and they'd know after our last visit to keep their cucumbers picked if they wanted them. Styx loves vegetables right off the vine.

Late Thursday evening, I took Styx for a special walk, explaining as we went that he'd be staying in Allport. Usually he travels with me, but the inn had a no-pets policy, and Styx is impossible to hide. In addition to his size, he gets excited in a new place, and within ten minutes everyone on my floor would know there was a dog somewhere.

We went to Styx's favorite park, which is on the opposite side of town. He liked it best because once, several years ago, he saw an elk there. Since dogs don't forget things like that, he's always on the lookout for another one. I enjoy the park too, because it edges Lake

Huron and the first stars come out right overhead, close enough that it seems you could reach up and prick your finger on their points.

Because I was looking at the stars, I missed it when Styx found a rotting carcass beside the trail. I think it was a woodchuck, but I didn't get close enough to find out for sure. By the time I realized what was happening he was on his back, squirming his big old body all around in it. "Styx! No!"

I was too late. When he stepped toward me, the stench hit my nose like a slap across the face. For once he didn't jump up for a hug, which kept me from actually vomiting. "Oh, Styx, you naughty boy!"

His beautiful brown eyes met mine, and he tilted his head to one side as if to ask, "What's wrong, Mom?"

Of course I couldn't be mad at him, but I also couldn't let him in my car—or take him to the Coulstons' in the morning—smelling like that. I slipped off his leash and pointed toward the lake. "Swim, Styx! Swim!"

He couldn't believe his luck. First a dead thing, and now an invitation to take a dip when he usually had to beg. Styx took off like a shot, his strong legs pumping through the sand. He hit the water full on, joyfully biting at waves that lapped along the shore. Soon he was swimming with strong strokes, visible only as a round knob and a muzzle sticking out of the water.

A bath would wash away most of the stink, I hoped. Of course I'd have a wet dog in the car on the way home, but I keep an old blanket in the back for just such occasions.

As I stood watching Styx swim, the leash rolled up in my hand, I thought about meeting Dina Engel. It would be fun to meet a clothing designer. What would she be like? Would we become friends? Would I have anything in common with the daughter of a drug king?

It was possible. Dina was launching a career in mid-life, perhaps due to the death of her mother. I'd been forced to change at about the same age when my beloved husband, a state police officer, was killed on the job. If Dina's urge to be a person of her own was real, we'd have things to talk about. If, on the other hand, it turned out she was part of her father's gang or posse or whatever they call it these days, I'd be happy to help take her down.

Hearing a noise down the beach, I turned. A man approached with a mid-sized dog, either a breed I didn't recognize or too many breeds to pick one. I'm not sure what made the dog decide I was a threat, but suddenly he lunged forward with a threatening growl. When I realized he wasn't on a leash, I had that flash of terror that comes when you have no idea what to do. The man shouted helplessly as the dog bounded toward me, teeth bared. If he'd been a Styx type, I'd have been in for a boisterous hug and slobber on my clothes. A horrible tension in my spine told me that wasn't what this dog intended.

The man shouted, "King! Get back here!" He might as well have whistled a happy tune. As the dog's paws ate up the ground between us, I tried to make a decision. Run? Stand firm? Crouch and protect my face with my arms?

The dog leaped, his powerful back legs pushing off and his body streamlining as he instinctively gauged the distance between us. In a millisecond I'd be at the mercy of those teeth. I could already feel the jaws closing on my arm, my shoulder, or even my throat. I opened my mouth to scream—

A blur to the right caught my eye. There was a thump as a large, furry object crossed the dog's path. His trajectory changed abruptly, and with a yelp of surprise, my attacker fell sideways onto the sand in a scramble of legs and tails. He lay there for a moment, stunned. Styx regained his feet and made a woof of mild outrage, as if to say any attack on his mom had to have been a mistake.

The dog whined once, rolled to his feet, and scurried back to his owner, who grabbed his collar and attached the leash that should have been in place all along. A decent person would have come over to apologize, but decent people don't have dogs that attack innocent walkers. The man tucked his chin into his chest and turned away, dragging the dog behind him.

It wasn't the first time Styx had saved me from pain and injury. The fact that he ended the event by shaking slightly stinky water all over me was a small price to pay.

"You're such a good boy," I told him. "Let's go see if the dog wash place is still open. You're the best, but you still smell like the worst."

Chapter Eight

Faye

The drive west was pleasant but twisty, since east-west travel in northern Lower Michigan usually involves a succession of different roads. We took US-23 to M-32, where we got on I-75 for a short time, exiting at Grayling to take M-72 to US-31 through Traverse City to pick up 22 north. There were a half-dozen other ways we might have chosen, but they all took about the same amount of time, and in summer contained the same amount of traffic, much of it out-of-state drivers either lost or distracted by the lovely views of trees, trees, and more trees. It paid to drive defensively, and Retta did.

We passed cherry orchards, apple orchards, and fields of sunflowers, in my opinion some of the happiest sights on earth. In Traverse City we stopped for cold drinks and visited Horizon Books, one of our favorites. I bought three new mystery novels, and Retta got a book on managing finances. She was good at minding the money she received after her husband's death, though there was no question she'd have given every cent away to have him back. I'm glad she's financially comfortable. I'm also glad I don't have enough money to make it necessary for me to do that kind of reading. Romance. Mystery. Nothing in the realm of reality for me.

North of Traverse City, a jut of land splits into two peninsulas that extend into Lake Michigan like tines on a mismatched barbeque fork. The inner one, Old Mission Peninsula, is short and thin, with a single road heading northward to a lighthouse that overlooks Grand Traverse Bay. The Leelanau Peninsula, our destination, is larger and offers more room for development. Temperate due to the water in and around it, the region is known for fruit-growing, including tart cherries, apples, and grapes for the many wineries located there. Often referred to as the "little finger of the Michigan mitten," the Leelanau begins with the Sleeping Bear Dunes National Lakeshore and continues thirty miles north past North and South Manitoulin Islands, ending at Leelanau State Park. One main road, M-22, serves the area, traveling up the west side almost to the point before turning to head down the opposite side and back to the city. Small local roads cut across at intervals, with signs listing places bound to be worth visiting, like Peshawbestown, an Ottawa/Chippewa enclave, or Cat Head Point, the estate of a former U. S. ambassador. "It's valued at six million," Retta told me, "in case you and Dale are looking for a place on the water."

Having never been up the peninsula, I was interested in the scenery. The weather people had promised a gorgeous few days, and despite their tendency to fib for the tourists, it was true this time. The land around us was deep, deep green, the water in the distance sparkled white on deep blue, and the sun shone yellow through the windows. The lakes kept the heat from becoming too oppressive, which was good, since Retta uses her A/C maybe twice a year. I hoped my deodorant served its purpose, but I hadn't thought to apply it down my spine or between my breasts.

For people used to a world of look-alike strip malls and drug stores on every corner, the Leelanau is appealing. There's plenty of open country interspersed with beautiful homes, charming cottages, and unique businesses. Tourists might stop along the tree-lined, two-lane road for ice cream cones then as they drive on have to brake to let a doe and her fawn step delicately onto the pavement and cross in front of the car.

St. Millicent's sat atop a low hill. Across the road and down a steep decline was the bay, and each front-facing room had a small balcony that promised a spectacular view of the sunrise. Behind the inn, the vineyard stretched to the west. To the south was a decidedly slanted parking lot, edged by woods that swept gracefully downhill.

As Retta pulled under the canopy, I gawked like the hick I am. Fronted with stone, the place was meant to look European, almost like old coach houses I'd seen in movies. At either side of the entrance sat wine barrels that appeared to be both old and authentic, though the winery itself was new. Two smiling valets approached and in seconds our luggage (my single suitcase and Retta's two plus a hanging rack, a makeup case, and a shoe bag) was piled on a cart. One valet explained that they preferred to park guests' cars due to the lot's steep angle. I guessed at some point an incautious visitor had failed to shift fully into park and ended up with his car in the trees.

Retta gave the young man a five-dollar bill and her car keys, and he thanked her graciously before driving fifty feet to a parking space. The other young man pulled the cart to the door then held it open for us, chatting cheerfully about the weather. I guessed he was aware that Retta had a stack of five-dollar bills in her bag just for charming, affable employees.

Inside, the lobby was paneled in old wood, lightened by strips of white limestone every few feet. The clerk was a fount of information, explaining amenities and offering extras like canoe rentals for lovers of the outdoors and spa treatments for those more content inside. Once we'd been assigned a room, our bags (and ten dollars!) disappeared up the stairs. We were directed to a common area down a short hallway, where Love-Able Ladies representatives welcomed us. Check-in had begun at ten, but Retta felt noon was the right time to arrive: not too eager-beaverish, but still on time for the opening events.

Lunch—I should say *luncheon*—was served at 12:30, and after waiting in the registration line, we made it just in time for the salad course. In the background, Teresa Brewer sang, "A Sweet Old-fashioned Girl." Nice touch.

The tables were set for ten, and most were full, but with her usual confidence Retta chose one where two side-by-side seats were available. "Mind if we join you, ladies?"

The women smiled in welcome, and Retta pointed to the chair I should take. She introduced us and began her entertaining line of patter while I tried to position myself far enough from the woman on my right to avoid bumping elbows.

I was already feeling anxious, and just walking into the room had been hard. It felt as if everyone looked up to check me out, and without Retta's casual acceptance of the attention, I'd have turned around and asked that nice young man to bring the car back right away. Now I sat silent, all too aware that our lunch companions were probably thinking I didn't belong there. I know it's dumb, but I can't help it.

When the salads (topped with dried cherries, an area specialty) were gone, the main course arrived. I soon realized that whatever else I left with, I was likely to take a few extra pounds home as well. The chicken salad sandwich (with more cherries) was served on a croissant (no calories there, right?) Dessert was five-layer chocolate cake with thick fudge frosting between layers. There was also a sampling of house wines, with a little spiel from the waiter about the two choices and a promise of more options at future meals.

I had to admit that Retta's clothing advice helped my confidence a little, though I'd resented it at the time. In my Marion's sale-rack red blouse, black pants (what else?), oversized white-on-gold necklace, and cut-out red flats, I didn't think I embarrassed my sister too badly. She'd even dragged me to her hair stylist for the first professional trim I'd had in years. Visibly uncertain of success, the woman had done what she could to tame my thick, wavy hair and added some gold highlights to "warm" my "look." She also gave me some "product" I was supposed to use to recreate the hairstyle after shampooing. (Yeah, right.) Still, it helped. I didn't feel like a princess yet, but I didn't feel quite so much like a frog.

Retta sparkled, but that's always the case. Not only was she born gregarious, she was a sort of goodwill ambassador for the Michigan State Police after Don's death, touring the state to speak on the need for better safety equipment for officers. Today she wore white leggings under a gorgeous, pale-yellow top, three necklaces ("One means nothing, two is mildly interesting, but three makes a statement"), dangly earrings, and a rattle-y bracelet. In minutes she'd charmed everyone at our table, explaining that we were "so very excited" to be at St. Millicent's and "just thrilled to meet others who enjoy being girls." I smothered a smile at the *Flower Drum Song* attitude, but our new friends ate it up.

The after-lunch speaker started things off with a bang, explaining that American society is falling apart due to gender confusion. Women, she told us, need to step back into their traditional roles in order to move the country in the right direction. "Look at history," she urged. "Every civilization that lived peacefully for any extended period had strong male leaders. Men provide the framework for a workable society. They make the rules, provide protection for weaker members, control finances, create healthy fiscal policies, and build impressive structures: roads, buildings, bridges, and machines. Women's roles are no less important, but they're less public. We nurture the next generation, maintain the home, and support the emotional needs of our men."

The argument that began in my head came in Barb's voice. Like the lawyer she'd been for decades, she'd have countered each point with logic. When the speaker claimed men aren't emotionally suited to be babysitters, Barb would have stood up and demanded, "How can a man 'babysit' his own children?" To the argument that women aren't suited for combat she'd have asked, "Exactly who is 'suited' to kill other people?" I didn't know enough history to be able to argue the claim that all strong societies are male-led, but I'd have bet Barb could name a dozen examples to dispute that claim.

The women around me applauded often, and I was glad Barb wasn't there to see it. The speaker claimed the world would be better off financially if women left the job market, since that would assure that every man in America was guaranteed employment. She cautioned us not to worry about the myth that today's family needed two incomes. "If women stop competing with men for jobs, the pay rate will rise as companies look at available workers. Prices will settle as the markets adjust, and all economic levels will end up with the same standard of living they have now. The added advantage will be a much stronger family unit, which will reduce crime, drug use, and many other problems our society now faces." She ended by urging each of us to "be happy with "your place in the world—under your man's strong arm."

Noting the enthusiastic applause, I realized these women rejected the teachings of the last sixty years. They were sick of hearing that being a wife and homemaker wasn't enough. They were tired of competing with men for jobs and advancement in those jobs. Maybe they'd seen their sisters try to work forty hours and still manage a house and taxi kids to after-school events, leaving no time for themselves. Love-Able Ladies preached that it was okay to be the lesser half of a couple, and these women seemed willing to let the men in their lives make all the decisions beyond what to serve for dinner. I understood it, though Barb never would. Security without responsibility was in many ways a tempting prospect. Was it best to let men be in charge? Were women fighting Nature when they insisted on equality?

The emcee—Angel—wrapped up the first meal of the weekend by urging us to chant with her three times: "Since I was born a girl, I'm going to be a *real* one!" The audience obeyed, sounding more determined each time. I made my mouth move and clapped politely, embarrassed by the demand for group participation.

As we left the banquet room, two-thirds of the crowd headed straight for the ladies' room. Touching my arm, Retta indicated a different direction. "We have a few minutes before the first session starts. Agent Auburn said to find him first chance we got."

"What's his cover?" Except for the valets and a couple of teenaged waiters, I'd seen only women in the hotel.

"He's posing as a limo driver, pretending to wait for someone in the back corner of the parking lot."

We left by the south-facing side doors, stepping into blinding sunshine and heat that was like an oven opened in our faces. On our left was the stunning view of the bay, and we both paused for a few seconds to take it in. To our right was the vineyard, where log benches had been placed along the first few rows to make pleasant seating for guests. We followed a limestone pathway to the parking lot, where Retta's Acadia sat between two similar models. She continued past it, heels dragging like little brakes against the slant. In the corner farthest from the road, under some trees that provided shade, was a black, square-looking car. Squinting a little, I saw there was someone in the driver's seat. His head lolled against the window, and his mouth hung slightly open. The FBI man was napping while he waited for us.

Except when we got to the car, Auburn wasn't asleep.

Retta realized it first, being a few steps ahead. I almost bumped into her as she gasped and stopped short. After a second of confusion I saw the ugly wound in a chest that was no longer rising and falling. We'd found a corpse where we'd expected an adviser.

We turned to each other in disbelief. "Is that—?"

She nodded. "Lars sent me a photo of the two of them fishing in the Gulf of Mexico." Retta opened her bag. "We need to call the police."

"Local or FBI?"

"The sheriff's department, I think. They'll bring in the FBI when they find out who he is."

She hadn't got her phone out when a man stepped from behind a panel truck. Slight and smaller than average in build, wearing skinny jeans, a sleeveless shirt, and a faint grin, he was handsome in a slightly greasy way. "You don't have to call anyone. I'll handle Agent Auburn."

Grabbing my sister's arm I said, "Run, Retta!"

But when we turned, a second man blocked our path. He was older than the first one, with gray stubble, salt-and-pepper hair, and clothes that looked as if he'd slept in them. A patch on his shirt identified him as an employee of St. Millicent's. He seemed confused, as if he'd come in late to the movie, and his demeanor lacked the hardness I saw in his companion. This guy was almost as scared as we were.

Flanked by the vehicles, we were blocked in. I was considering a leap over the hood of Auburn's car when Retta tapped my arm and pointed. The first man had drawn a gun. He held the weapon low, so a casual glance across the parking lot would reveal only two women talking to two men. Our body language might have telegraphed fear, but most of the attendees were by this time trooping into a session on one of two topics: *Beauty after Fifty* or *Tone That Midsection!* The staff was clearing away lunch. It wasn't likely anyone would see us.

"What are you two doing out here?"

I couldn't think of a thing to say, but Retta came up with a pretty good lie. "My sister wanted a cigarette before our session."

"Why'd you come all the way over here?"

"There's a sign." Retta pointed to where there was indeed a notice asking people to move away from the doorways to smoke.

He wasn't sure he bought it, but Retta can look so darned innocent that it's hard to believe she's capable of a lie. The gun-toter spoke, possibly to his partner but more likely to himself. "What are we gonna do with them?"

The older man shifted his feet, apparently worried about the answer. I guessed he hoped it wouldn't be the same thing they'd done with Agent Auburn. Since he had no gun, it wasn't likely his opinion held much sway with the younger man.

"They ain't cops." He looked at us. "You ain't cops, are you?"

"No, we're not," Retta said firmly.

"Don't mean nothing," the younger man said. "They saw him."

"I don't know why you did that anyway, I mean—"

"Shut up." His tone would have done it, but the order was accompanied by a look that made the older man press his lips together.

"I guess we could put them in the back of the Feeb's car and let them ride into Lake Michigan with him."

The man in the inn's staff shirt clearly didn't like that idea. "They're s'posed to be at this lady-thing, Tr—"

"No names!" the guy with the gun interrupted.

His head drooped. "Sorry. It's just when I talk to people, I like to say their name."

"Then pick a fake one."

The older man's brow furrowed. "Like what?"

"Who cares?" The blond guy jerked the thumb of his gun-free hand in our direction. "They don't need to know nothing about us."

"How about Ted and Bill?"

"What?"

"Like in the movie. *Bill and Ted's Excellent Adventure.*"

The handsome one shook his head scornfully. "Fine. I'm Ted, you're Bill."

"Okay, Ted. What if somebody asks where these ladies went?"

"They won't find them."

"Yeah, but guests disappearing would mess up the weekend for, um, somebody."

"Right." 'Ted' was reluctant. "I better ask. Hold this." Glaring a warning as he reached between us, he handed the gun to his companion. 'Bill' held it as if it were a grenade with the pin already pulled.

Though part of my mind screamed that death was imminent, another part noticed the lightning speed with which Ted texted. I think each generation alters genetically, adapting to technology without conscious awareness of capabilities it has that older people don't. Aside from Retta, I don't know anyone over fifty who doesn't labor over every letter of a text message.

As we waited for a response, Retta met my gaze and raised her brows, indicating she had no idea what to do next. I couldn't fault her for that, because neither did I.

The phone pinged, and the guy read the message. "Huh."

"What?" the older guy said. I thought of him as "older" only in the sense that he was closer to our age than to his pal's.

"We need to make sure the fashion show goes on Sunday like it's planned." Ted's manner indicated he was quoting an authority figure. "If these ladies keep their mouths shut about what they saw, nobody at the FBI will know Auburn isn't on the job."

Bill rolled his eyes. "So we ask them nice not to tell they saw a corpse in the parking lot?"

Ted responded with a greasy grin. "I think one of them is starting to feel a little sick. She's going to spend the weekend in her room while the other one attends the conference."

The wheels spun in Bill's head, but nothing shifted into gear. "I don't get it."

"You chaperone the sick one, and the other one makes excuses downstairs." His tone changed to what I interpreted as an attempt to sound truthful while telling a lie. "Once things are wrapped up here, we let them go."

Though he liked the last part, Bill had a question. "I'm going to spend the weekend in a hotel room with these two?"

"Until I say different." Ted turned to Retta. "What's your room number?"

"Two-ten."

"You each got a key?" She nodded and he ordered, "Give me yours." When she complied, he spoke to me. "Do whatever you're supposed to do at these things, and make it look like everything is okay. If anyone asks, your sister feels real bad, but you paid good money to come here so you're going ahead as planned." He poked a finger in my face. "You got that?"

I tried twice before my voice worked. "Y-yes."

"I picked you because this one looks like a schemer to me, and we don't want none of that. Do like I tell you and we'll be gone on Sunday. After that you can tell anybody you want to. Got it?"

"Yes."

"Good." He turned back to Bill. "You understand what you're going to do?"

"Yeah, but I'm supposed to be working."

"Doing what?"

Ted surveyed the trees around us. "The boss said to work away from the inn so I don't bother the ladies. I was gonna trim some trees."

"Perfect. They won't expect to see you very often."

Ted's expression revealed doubt. "Are you sure—"

"Just do what you're told," Ted interrupted. "Now help me get this body out of the driver's seat." He set the gun on the running board of the truck, within easy reach. "You two stand in front of the car so nobody sees what we're doing."

Feeling like I was in a horror movie, I stood near the grill of Auburn's car, pretending to chat with Retta while Ted laid the front seat down. Grunting and swearing, he and Bill dragged the body into the back. As Retta and I tried not to look, the seat returned to upright position with a grind. Ted got in, turned the key, and rolled down the window. "Don't screw this up."

"I won't." Bill sounded less sure than his words indicated.

Ted thought about things for a few seconds. "Take their phones, and check the room for tablets or laptops or whatever. We don't want them sending any messages."

Ted had also begun to consider the practicalities of the situation. "How am I s'posed to march them inside with a gun in my hand? What if we meet somebody?"

"For cryin' out loud!" Ted got out, opened the trunk, and dug around in Auburn's overnight case. "Here. Wear this, and put the gun in the pocket." He tossed a black hoodie at Bill, who caught it clumsily.

As he twisted the gun through the armhole, I worried for a few seconds that one of us would be shot through sheer ineptitude. I hoped if that happened, it would be Ted who stopped a bullet.

He apparently had the same thought. "Geez! Didn't you ever handle a gun before?"

"Sure." Bill settled the gun in the pocket. "I just never thought I'd aim one at a person."

Disgusted, Ted got back into the car and rammed it into gear. The sound of the limo's engine receded to a purr as he pulled smoothly onto the roadway and headed north.

Once he was gone, Bill seemed to pull courage from somewhere inside. "Take me to your room," he ordered, "so I can see how we're gonna do this."

As we approached the inn, I wondered if anyone would ever learn what happened to FBI agent Chet Auburn. Unless we worked very hard to avoid it, I was pretty sure Retta and I would eventually join him in the waters of Grand Traverse Bay.

Chapter Nine

Barb

Retta is a texter, so as soon as my sisters arrived at St. Millicent's I got a message letting me know. I texted back *Have Fun!* with a sarcastic emoji. I knew she'd enjoy herself: it was social; it was girly; there was free wine. On the other hand, Faye would find herself wishing she were out of there by bedtime tonight—noon tomorrow at the latest.

My stomach told me it was lunchtime, so I pushed myself away from the computer and went to see what Faye had left us to eat while she was gone. Her dog Buddy raised his head hopefully when he heard footsteps but sank dejectedly to the floor when he saw it was me. I felt a moment of pity for him. Buddy had been Faye's constant companion since she rescued him on the road more than a year before, and it's hard to explain to a dog that his life's focus is only gone for the weekend, not forever.

"She'll be back soon," I told him, bending to pat him on the head.

The reward for my kindness was a snarl and a snap. Instinctively I pulled my hand back, though Buddy had no intention of biting me. He just wanted to let me know I could not replace Faye in his life.

"Jerk."

My brother-in-law stood before the open refrigerator door, surveying the insane amount and variety of food choices Faye had prepared for us in the apparent belief we were incapable of sustaining ourselves. I glimpsed stacked plastic containers with labels like sloppy joes, tuna casserole, and broccoli-bacon salad.

Having heard my exchange with Buddy, Dale commented, "That dog's all Faye's. I'm lucky he lets me be in the same room."

I grimaced but had to be fair about it. "My cat isn't the friendliest of pets either."

He chuckled. "Now that's the truth, but it's because you've spoiled her. She used to take whatever she could get. Now the critter won't even take a bite of tuna from me."

When a stray cat started coming to my bedroom window some months before, I'd coaxed her into a relationship. Nowadays, Brat inhabited my upstairs apartment, going and coming on the roof when it pleased her and refusing to visit the downstairs under any circumstances. I'd made one attempt to introduce her, carrying her down in my arms, but when she and Buddy saw each other the result was a growl, a hiss, a frenzied scramble back upstairs, and a nasty scratch on my arm. Most days Brat dozed in sunny corners of my sitting room, and at night she slept at the foot of my bed. Having figured out that having a human meant free food, she ventured outside only often enough to keep her hunting skills sharp.

Dale set several containers on the table while I got out plates and silverware. "People find the pet that suits them," he said, "or maybe vice versa. Faye likes to be needed, and Buddy sure did when she found him on the road. Styx craves affection, which Retta's got lots of to give. Your cat wants her independence and her dignity, like you."

Though I was a little surprised at Dale's shrewd analysis, he was correct. While all the Evans girls are fairly independent, I'm the one who most resists leaning on others. Our mother was that way, a self-possessed woman who was kind-hearted but hardly emotionally effusive. Her joys were shared with serenity; her pain was kept to herself.

A memory rose in my mind of the only time I ever knew of that my mother broke down and cried, really cried. I remembered it clearly, because it was my fault.

As her oldest, I was like a friend to Mom in many ways. We shared opinions, gossip, and dreams while Retta played with Barbies and Faye helped Dad with the animals. When I left home for the University of Michigan, Mom had been very proud. Still, Dad had told me privately that she was lonely without me. When I announced I wasn't coming home for the summer but instead moving in with my boyfriend, Mom said nothing. Later that day, I heard her crying in her room. I guessed that was when she realized we'd never again be as close as we'd once been. Though I told myself she still had Dad and my sisters, I never forgot that day, when my mother's tears came from what I'd done.

Dale closed the refrigerator door, bringing me back to the present. "I hope the girls are having fun," I said. "They must be busy, because Retta just sent one short text."

He frowned. "I tried to call Faye a while ago. She had some papers I was supposed to give Gabe and Mindy, but I can't find the envelope." Our once-in-a-while agency go-fer and his new wife had launched a project to benefit senior citizens in the area, and we supported their efforts when we could. Spooning portions from several containers onto his plate Dale mused, "I wanted to ask her where it is, but I guess Faye turned off her phone so it wouldn't disrupt the meetings. It went right to voicemail. I don't think she sent an answer."

He handed me his phone, and I confirmed that Faye hadn't sent a message. Dale could make calls and check the weather with his phone, but that was all. Handing his phone back, I took my own from my pocket. "I'll text Retta and ask her to have Faye call you."

While we waited, I had some of the broccoli salad. Dale finished his lunch and got some cookies from the breadbox. When we each had eaten a cookie and still hadn't heard anything I said, "I'll try her voice mail." Retta didn't answer, so I called and left a short message. "She'll feel it pulse, even if she's got the sound turned off."

As we waited, we chatted idly about the beautiful weather and the chores we each had planned for the afternoon. As always, Dale was funny in a gentle way, pointing out life's absurdities without coming off as bitter or angry. I enjoyed the meal and his company.

Though our arrangement was what some might consider odd, I like having Dale and Faye live with me. When I returned to Allport in 2014, they'd been in rough shape financially. Dale received monthly disability payments from a work-related injury, but his portion of his medical bills was considerable. Faye had worked all her life at small offices, but citing the tough economy, her last boss had let her go. In addition, one of their three sons always seemed to need financial help, which had left Faye, at almost fifty, struggling to stay afloat. Knowing it would be difficult to find a new job at her age, she'd suggested we start a detective agency. At first I told her she was crazy, but she'd kept at it until I agreed, partly to help her and partly from a need for something to do. As soon as Faye and I got started, little sister Retta insisted on becoming part of it. Some days that was good; other days less so.

Since I never married, I'd suggested Faye, Dale, and I share the big old house I bought a few blocks from Allport's downtown. We ran our agency from two rooms at the front that had once been parlors. Faye and Dale took the other four rooms downstairs as living space, including the kitchen, where Faye excels and I don't. I lived upstairs in an apartment I painted off-white and left largely undecorated, suiting my Spartan tastes.

The offer had been made to make my sister's life easier, so it was a bonus for me to find that Dale and I got along well. He recognized our sister bond, odd because of our different life experiences but firm nonetheless, and he was never jealous of the time we spent together. Dale's days were mostly spent in a shed in the back yard, where he repaired small engines for locals who lacked either the patience or the know-how to do it. When circumstances demanded, he was willing to man the office and answer the land line so we were free to pursue leads. He accepted that running the agency was what Faye wanted to do, though I knew he worried about our safety. Several times over the last three years, his worry had been completely justified.

If the subject of danger arose Faye made a joke, contending she'd rather die taking action than languish to a ripe old age in a nursing home. Dale always smiled and shook his head when she started in. "We don't get to choose," he'd tell her. "If we did, we'd all come with an off-switch." Dale and Faye were one of those lucky couples meant for each other, and they kept going forward together despite the tragedies they faced. I was often a little jealous, though I'd had my moments.

I touched the necklace I wore almost every day, given to me by the man who'd have been my mate for life if ALS hadn't killed him. A second chance at love had arrived with the local police chief, though we agreed it was too late for wedding bells and setting up housekeeping together.

As if he'd read my mind Dale asked, "Rory's not around today?"

"He's visiting his daughter," I replied.

"Guess Allport can do without him for a few days." Dale helped himself to another of the oatmeal cookies Faye had left us and shoved the bowl toward me. I shook my head. In mid-life, every cookie counts against you.

He rose, taking a third cookie for the road. "I'm almost finished with Terry Cantrell's motorbike, so I guess I'll get back to it."

"So we'll get to hear that angry bumblebee whine up and down our street again soon?" I asked glumly.

Dale winked. "I put a muffler on it. The kid isn't smart enough to figure out how to get it off, so the neighborhood should be a little quieter from now on."

Chapter Ten

Faye

Ted ushered Retta and me through the side door we'd exited earlier, keeping one hand on the gun in his jacket pocket. Though Bill wasn't much of a tough-guy, when there's a gun involved I tend to do as I'm told. I hoped we'd meet someone who asked what he was up to, since two scared-looking women preceded a man wearing a jacket on a day when it was eighty-five degrees outside. There was no one around.

Once we were inside our hotel room, Bill ordered us to sit on the small couch near the window. Placing himself between us and the door, he consulted the conference schedule. "You'll go down to dinner at six," he told me. "Tell people your sister isn't feeling good and ask for her dinner to be brought up here."

"If I were sick, I wouldn't want anything to eat," Retta told him.

"*I* need to eat."

"Well, you're not getting my supper."

"I'll get what I say."

Retta raised her nose a little. "We'll split it."

After glaring at her for a few seconds, Bill turned to me. "Say she hurt her back taking stuff out of her trunk."

"I didn't bring in my own suitcase," Retta said. "That's what valets are for."

Bill looked grumpy at being corrected a second time. "She don't know how she hurt it, but she can't stand up."

"If I were in that much pain, I'd go to a doctor."

His jaw jutted. "Today you're going to suffer in silence, because you spent all this money to come here. You're hoping it gets better overnight." He pointed at Retta's nose. "But it ain't gonna, so get used to these four walls."

We lapsed into an uneasy silence that was interrupted by static coming from a radio attached to Bill's belt. "Maintenance? Where are you?"

The look on his face said he wasn't pleased to get a call, but he removed the radio from his belt and answered, "Uh, out back."

"Can you make a run to the store? We're out of some things."

His face twisted, and it was obvious he couldn't think of a plausible lie. To my surprise, Retta pantomimed turning an imaginary screwdriver.

Bill got it. "I got the lawnmower all torn apart and—" Now Retta seemed to be putting on gloves, but he understood. "There's grease all over me. Somebody else better go."

"Okay," the caller said with a sigh. "I guess I can go." When the transmission ended, Bill looked relieved and Retta seemed pleased. I rolled my eyes at her misplaced kindness: aid and comfort to the enemy. She gave me half a wink, and I realized what she was up to. Retta was trying to get Bill, the weaker of our two captors, on our side.

Rising, Bill fetched the TV remote, and soon we were watching a *Gilligan's Island* rerun. Of the three of us, one thought the show was hilarious.

Before I left the room at six, Bill gave me a long list of mostly useless instructions. He warned that someone would be watching me, so I shouldn't do anything "goofy." I wasn't sure if he was lying or not, but as I went down the stairs to the open area, it felt like everyone below looked up from their wineglasses to notice me.

As I surveyed the crowd below, I wondered who among them was watching me for reasons more sinister than judging my fashion IQ. Something that was supposed to happen on Sunday couldn't be threatened, but what? Had Ted killed an FBI agent to keep him from disrupting a fashion show? Where was the response from the rest of the FBI? If Auburn had come alone, how long would it take for his people to become worried and start north to investigate?

What was going to happen during the show or immediately afterward? I thought, quite naturally, of kidnapping. Dina Engel's father was very wealthy. Did that mean she was in danger? If kidnapping was the plan, why had Ted killed Auburn? My mind was going in circles. I simply didn't know enough to make a decision, much less a plan. I started down the steps, determined to learn what I could about everyone I met during the evening.

In the dining room, women were choosing seats for dinner. The hum of conversation was underscored by the soft clink of wine glasses filled and set before willing tasters. I felt a wave of nervousness, almost nausea, at the prospect of joining one of the groups and pretending to be at ease among them. To keep Retta safe, I had to. I'd been given a part to play, and I had to face these strangers—alone and with confidence. Pasting on a smile, I approached a table and asked, "May I join you?"

The women were obliging, and I told my story of arriving with my sister only to have her back go out. "I got her some ibuprofen," I concluded. "We hope she'll be okay in the morning."

"Isn't that the way it goes?" one of my tablemates said. "You look forward to something then Life reaches out and slaps you in the face."

They began telling stories related to that theme. Apparently listening, I glanced around the room, searching for Dina Engel. If I could locate her, I would introduce myself somehow and try to figure out if she was the target of an impending plot, the reason for the plot, or completely separate from the plot.

At the front of the room was the VIP table. The woman who'd spoken at lunch (which seemed like years ago) was there, along with conference director Angel Sonora, who seemed on edge. Twice I saw her excuse herself to tend to some issue. Once she spoke to the waiter in charge of the crew, and he went off in a purposeful manner to relay the message to the others. The second time she went to the doorway, where an ancient but expensively-dressed woman tottered in on the arm of a younger one, perhaps a relative. Angel led them to her table, where two chairs had been tilted against the table to signify reservation. When the old woman was seated, Angel returned to her chair. Though she hardly touched her meal, she made bright chatter with her guests, smiling at each one an equal number of times, as far as I could judge. A well-run conference apparently means a lot of stress for the person in charge.

The last chair at the table remained empty until just before the main course was served. When a woman slipped past the waiter and took it, I recognized Dina Engel from the picture we'd found online. She looked surprisingly normal for a fashion maven: simple white pants, a pale pink top cut longer in back, and soft flats that offered nothing in the way of foot support. Her hair was longer than it had been in the picture, falling softly onto her shoulders. As the salad plates were cleared, the woman next to Dina made large gestures as she spoke. Though she didn't have much to say in return, she listened attentively.

Catching a look of concern on the face of one of my tablemates, I realized I hadn't touched my salad, which had been removed and replaced with a plateful of food. Once again we'd been given enough to feed a roomful of lumberjacks, a braised, marinated pork tostada with grilled pineapple and a black bean salsa. It was paired with a Pinot Noir, according to the placard at my place-setting. I ate a little and tried to seem as delighted with it as everyone else at my table was.

As we ate, one of the women shared her current family crisis, which in my opinion should have been nobody's business. Her daughter was pregnant by a man who had no job and who treated her, in her mother's words, "like a dirty rag."

"I couldn't stop crying the whole month of June," she confided. "We've given that girl everything, and she's throwing it all away."

"It's like the speaker said at lunch," another woman opined. "These feminist types have destroyed all sense of family. How can society remain strong when girls have babies by one man this year and a different man next year? Some of my friends wouldn't know their grandchildren if they met them at the mall."

The others commiserated, tutting and tsking about ungrateful children who have no idea what their parents have sacrificed for them. "I remember when getting pregnant outside marriage was a shame," one said. "Now you see girls walk across the stage at graduation and you hope they don't deliver before they get to the other side."

I kept my eyes on my plate, but her words brought to mind the only time I saw my mother cry. It was toward the end of my senior year when I told her I was pregnant for Jimmy. I moved in with Dale soon after and graduated high school with a barely discernible baby bulge. Mom never said out loud that it hurt her, but I never forgave myself for making my strong, wonderful mother cry.

As the desserts were being served (cheesecake with fresh blackberries in a sweet sauce), we were introduced to our special guest for the evening, Rosalind Rayburn. It was the old woman I'd noticed earlier, and when the emcee gave her bio I realized I'd read a few of her books decades ago. Rosalind was one of the early "bodice-ripper" authors, romance novels with plenty of adventure, sex, and adventurous sex. She was now nearly ninety, and her grand-daughter and heir apparent had come along to do the speaking.

In her speech, "Free from Feminism," Robin Rayburn spoke at length about how romance novels allow women to use their imaginations and therefore become more complete as women. The heroines, she explained, don't try to be like men. They remain fully female yet achieve their goals through perseverance and (she really used this word, I swear) *pluck.*

Taken for what they were, I couldn't say Rosalind's books were bad. Still, I was aware Barb would have had plenty to say if she were here. *What goals do the characters have other than marriage? Do a woman's problems magically disappear when the right man chooses to make her his wife? And even if they do, is it worth giving up her right to be who she is?*

Retta, on the other hand, would have said it was all in good fun, and only the silliest of us believe there's anything realistic about Scottish lairds finding mysterious women on the heaths or New York millionaires needing a convenient bride, no questions asked.

Reminded of Retta, I considered borrowing a phone, hiding in the rest room, and calling for help. The question that stopped me was whether the local police had the know-how and the resources to rescue her before Ted or Bill killed her. It was hard to say. I might call Barb, but what could she do? The FBI should be informed of Agent Auburn's murder, but again, I might start a chain of events that would end with my sister's death. Apparently adjusting my chair, I glanced around the room. Their confederate was supposedly watching me, so I decided I couldn't take the chance until I knew more. Which led me back to my earlier plan: approach Dina Engel and assess her involvement.

When people began to make their way to the pool area for the wine-tasting, I went toward Dina's table, where I heard her tell her companions she intended to head upstairs and get some sleep. It wasn't easy for me to introduce myself to a complete stranger, but when she stepped away from the others I approached and asked, "Are you the fashion designer?"

Dina looked past me as she answered, and I imagined her wishing she'd left a few seconds sooner. "That's me."

"I'm Faye Burner, and I love what I saw of your stuff on the Detroit Chic website." It was probably a mistake to call it *stuff*, but it was a lie anyway. Most days I put on stretch jeans and an oversized t-shirt and call myself dressed.

"Thanks." She was hard to read: shy? Uninterested? Since I'd pinned my hopes on her reacting with pleasure at meeting a fan, I was at a loss as to how to continue. "I can't wait for the show on Sunday."

A hint of nervousness showed on her face, and she answered with unexpected honesty. "I'll be glad when it's over."

It wasn't a ringing statement of confidence, but if I were a former stay-at-home about to launch a project that had captured the attention of relevant media and interested females all over the state, I might be feeling a little jittery too. Dina probably should have developed nerves of steel from living with a man who courted arrest daily, but I supposed this was different, more personally scary.

I'd noticed she seemed to be alone. "You probably have a lot to do before Sunday. Will you have help?"

She gave me an assessing look. "My father is sending someone."

"That's good."

I got a second look. "I'm sure you're right."

Okay, Faye, I told myself. *You aren't exactly a skilled interrogator, and this woman has no doubt practiced not telling anyone anything personal for decades. Give it up.*

We parted at the door. I headed upstairs to our room, anxious to be sure Retta was okay but faintly bothered by my exchange with Dina. For a woman whose lifelong dream was about to come true, she seemed more anxious than excited. Was she nervous because she knew an FBI agent had been murdered? I couldn't decide what the woman's manner told me. Was she afraid for her show, for herself, or for something else?

Chapter Eleven

Retta

You picture being kidnapped as a terrifying experience, and for the first few minutes, it was. But once Ted, the more dangerous of our two captors, left to dispose of the corpse he'd created, we had only Bill to deal with, and he was no killer. There was the gun Ted had given him, but he seemed half afraid of it. As long as we did what he said, I figured we were safe. Over the course of the afternoon, Bill repeated several times that we'd be released when the retreat ended. I could tell Faye didn't believe that, but he insisted it was true. "You don't know our real names, so why should we care if you girls call the police after we're gone?"

I could think of several answers to that question. They'd killed Agent Auburn, which indicated life wasn't exactly precious to them. Bill was employed by the inn, so if we reported he was in on the murder the police could track him using the information they had on him. We could give detailed descriptions of each man. Overall, it wasn't in their best interests to set us free.

What were Bill and Ted doing here, and whose side were they on? If they were guarding Dina, Ted must have thought Auburn posed some kind of threat, but why murder him? If they weren't bodyguards sent by Roger Engel, they might be part of some rival gang that planned to kidnap Dina or even kill her. Aside from the vague reference to the fashion show and the command from someone higher up the chain of command that it not be interrupted, I had no inkling of what was going on. Ted hadn't been willing to share information, and Bill didn't seem to have any. We'd have to wait and see.

After Faye went to dinner, an uneasy silence hung between Bill and me. He watched yet another old sitcom, casting sideways glances in my direction from time to time. We both tensed when someone rapped on the door softly, but right afterward came, "Room service, ma'am." Bill disappeared into the bathroom, motioning with his head as he went to indicate I should answer.

I'd already been told what to do, so I opened the door with my back bent in what looked like a painful wrench. A young woman holding a tray said, "We hear you're having a bad time."

Backing away in my crumpled state, I let her enter and set the tray on the counter. "I hope to be back to normal tomorrow."

"If there's anything else we can do, just give us a call," she said. I gave her the tip I had in hand, already checked by Bill to make sure it was only a couple of dollar bills. She left, wishing me a good night's sleep and a better day on Saturday.

Ted emerged from the bedroom and went directly to the tray of food. "What have we got here?" Lifting the silver plate cover, he revealed a chicken breast smothered with melted cheese, three spears of asparagus, and four baby redskin potatoes. Off to one side was a bowl of spinach salad with what looked like raspberry vinaigrette dressing. On the opposite side was a yummy-looking slab of Victorian walnut cake. Two small carafes sat beside an empty wineglass and a tumbler. I peered into one; it was iced tea. Bill sniffed at the other and said, "Wine. I don't know what kind."

"White Zin, I'd guess. My sister knows what I like."

Bill frowned. "Doesn't look like much for two people."

I thought about saying I hadn't exactly invited him to dinner. Still, the man had to eat. "I'm not fond of asparagus," I told him. "You can have that, and I'll eat the salad." He opened his mouth to say something then closed it. "And that big slab of cheese is too much for me. I'll eat the chicken and you can have the cheese, so we both get protein to fill us up." I considered the rest of the meal. "You get the potatoes—too starchy—and I'll take the cake. I'm sure you don't want the wine, which would make you sleepy, so you get the iced tea." Bill looked doubtful, but it was a fifty-fifty split, as least as far as I could manage.

He made a move toward the fork, but I got to it first and handed him the teaspoon. Moving the cake to a napkin, I transferred the asparagus, potatoes, and cheese onto its small plate. "Those potatoes do look good," I said. "Do you mind if I just see how they taste?"

Though his frown said he did, Bill held the plate while I speared a quarter of his starches. "Thank you," I said. The world is a nicer place when you're polite, even to kidnappers.

"So you're supposed to be working on the grounds," I said as we ate. "What happens if they go looking and don't find you?"

"It'd take a while before they got suspicious," he replied. "I'm the only maintenance guy, so I'm all over the property. They can call on the radio, but it ain't like it's got GPS." He grinned. "Sometimes I pretend I'm out of range when I don't want to answer."

"What if someone needs to see you in person?"

The frown returned. "I gotta figure that out. Tomorrow I'm supposed to meet with the fashion show people and help them get ready for Sunday." Squaring his narrow shoulders he explained, "I done some work for the Cherry Festival a few years back, so I know about sound and that."

"Then you can't spend all weekend in this room."

"No." He shook it off. "But Tr-Ted will figure it out. He says they pay him to think and they pay me to do what he says."

I wanted to say he really should do a little thinking for himself, but I guessed it wouldn't help. Instead I finished off the cake, which was amazing.

When we'd finished eating, Bill set the tray out in the hallway and went back to watching TV. I sat on the bed, contemplating the oddity of my situation.

I had been kidnapped by criminals—murderers. I should be in tears, shaking like a leaf and cowering in a corner. But it was hard to be afraid with my captor watching *I Dream of Jeannie* and chuckling at Barbara Eden's antics.

Besides, the Evans girls aren't much for crying.

Lying on my side on the bed, I let my mind wander back over the years. I'd never seen Barbara Ann cry. Faye had had plenty to cry about over the years, but she never surrendered to tears for long. Me? I'd done my share when Don died, but since then, not much.

If our dad ever felt like crying he never showed it, and I remember Mother crying only once, when I was in high school. When it was over, she refused to talk about why she'd been so sad. I remember it because I'd gotten a Minor in Possession citation the weekend before and was kicked off the Honor Society because of it.

I always wondered what Faye or Barbara Ann did to make our mother cry.

Chapter Twelve

Faye

It was almost eight when the after-dinner speaker, who was all for chastity until marriage, let us go. When I got back to the room, Retta and I had no chance to speak privately, but she appeared to be all right. In fact, she and Bill had an exchange that might have been funny in different circumstances. He sat in the lone upholstered chair while she half-reclined on the bed, every pillow in the room piled behind her for back support. When the TV show they were watching ended, Retta said, "It's my turn to choose."

Bill looked at her like she'd just swatted him with one of the pillows. "Your turn?"

She gave him a one-brow-raised look, which is when Retta most resembles Barb. "Didn't your parents teach you about taking turns?"

"Well, yeah."

"Do you think it's fair that you chose every single show since we got here?"

Bill's brow furrowed as he considered that, and Retta went on with the assurance she always exhibits when explaining why you're wrong. "All afternoon we watched re-runs from the '60s and '70s, and I didn't object. Now it's prime time, and there are decent shows on." Taking up the remote, she navigated to the guide and scrolled for a few seconds. "Have you seen *Orphan Black?* I think you'd really like it. "

Bill's lips moved, repeating the title without voice, and his forehead creased as he groped for a response. Would he get angry at Retta's audacity and remind her he was the one with a gun?

"I guess." And they settled in to watch Sarah's latest adventure.

Uninterested in fictional accounts of TV troubles, I settled on the second bed with my back to the room, ostensibly reading a novel. In truth I was trying to figure out what we'd stumbled into and how we might escape. My first thought was a plot to kidnap Dina, perhaps to put pressure on Engel or avenge something he'd done. But why would that happen during the fashion show, when she'd be surrounded by people? Why not now, when she seemed to be on her own?

The show might be a cover for some other crime, like robbery. There were plenty of well-off women at the retreat, and Bill and Ted might plan to burgle their rooms while they were oohing and ahhing over Dina's designs. Maybe. Maybe. Maybe.

At eleven Bill took out his phone and made a call. "Where are you?" He listened then said, "Okay, but you need to stay with the ladies in the morning so I can at least pretend I'm doing my work."

As he listened, his jaw jutted. "It ain't baby-sitting. It's guarding, and I did my share." He glanced at us. "I can't even use the john, man."

More listening. "I know you did. Did it, um, did it go okay?" … "Sure, sure, I get it. So are you going to come here and help out or what?" … "Okay, okay. I was just asking."

He stabbed the disconnect button with more force than was necessary, mumbling something that had the word *jerk* in it.

Retta was instantly sympathetic. "He doesn't understand how hard this is for you."

"He don't. I mean, I know he's got stuff to do too, but jeez."

"Listen," Retta said. "We can handle the problem you mentioned pretty easily."

"Problem?"

"You need to visit the little boys' room, right?"

Bill's face flushed. "I—um—yeah, I guess so."

"Here's what we'll do. Faye and I will sit on the bed, facing the window. We promise not to look, and you can do what you need to do with the bathroom door open. We can even turn up the TV so the, um, sounds are covered."

He glanced around the room, assessing her offer. The bathroom was near the door, so he would remain between us and escape. "Okay."

As we turned our backs, I wondered if Retta had a plan. Were we supposed to wait until Bill was fully occupied and make a break for it? It would have to be both of us, and we'd have to be really quick. I looked at her for a sign, but she simply sat there, facing the window as she'd promised. She even whistled softly, covering the sound of water on water that was audible even over the weather girl's predictions.

I heard a zipper, and Bill came back into the room. "Uh, thanks."

"No problem," Retta told him sweetly. "Maybe you'll do something nice for us sometime."

Bill set his chair across the passageway to the door, turned off the lights, and told us in an almost kindly manner to get some sleep. I turned my back and pretended to sleep. After a while I heard soft snoring and turned hopefully to look. His snuffling sounds were the kind of settling-in noises that often wake the snorer, not the deep breathing of real sleep. In the soft light from the window the gun was plainly visible, wedged between the buttons of his shirt like an oversized tie tack. Though his method of keeping it handy would be frowned upon by any self-respecting weapons trainer, I saw no way to sneak up on him without getting shot for my efforts. Maybe later in the night, when he slept more deeply, his hand would fall away and I could snatch the gun before he woke and stopped me. I wasn't particularly optimistic about that prospect, but it was the only hopeful thought I had.

Chapter Thirteen

Retta

I figured out right away that Bill was a lot like Gerald, a kid I'd known in seventh grade. Because he wanted so badly to be liked, Gerald would do whatever the guys in eighth grade told him to. He plugged up the toilets in the boys' bathroom with paper toweling and jammed the lock of the history classroom door with pencil lead while the teacher was at lunch. Every time, the older boys told him it would be cool and he'd never get caught, but every time, someone saw him in the vicinity or word got around to the principal, and he did. Everyone but me thought it was hilarious that Gerald always got in trouble but kept doing dumb stuff anyway. Gerald would accept his punishment like he'd been given an award, because he thought his fellow students admired his daring. Instead, they laughed at his cluelessness.

In the spring of that year, I took Gerald on as a project. He really was a sweet guy, but his parents were drunks who provided no guidance at all. I wanted Gerald to see he was just entertainment for the mean kids, but of course you can't just tell someone that. I began by chatting with him in classes we shared, asking about his new Wranglers or if he liked Olivia Newton-John's new song. Once we got to know each other a little, I worked on convincing him he didn't need to show off for the others. I said his drawings of Vikings and monsters were really interesting, and after a while I invited him to hang out with me and my friends at lunchtime. Every day from then on he waited at the lunch room door for me, ready to carry my tray or run for whatever I might have forgotten, like a spoon or some milk.

My friends didn't get it, and I admit Gerald didn't fit in very well. He was geeky and immature and kept interjecting comments about what Thor would do in a certain situation. Still, he listened to every word I said like I was Freyja herself, and he was ready to do whatever I suggested. He stopped being the school prankster and, with my encouragement, started doing his homework and passing his tests. He ignored the rolled eyes and subtle sarcasms of the others at the table or in the bleachers at the basketball games, focusing only on me and what I wanted.

Things got a little uncomfortable when Gerald started showing up at our house, but he never minded that I had other things to do. On Saturdays he'd hitchhike or walk out to the farm then hang out in the barn with Dad or help Mom in the garden. He became like another pet, and we had plenty of those. Despite his immaturity and lack of manners, Mom and Dad included Gerald in whatever they were doing that day. Barbara ignored him, but she always had her nose stuck in a book anyway. If I was on the phone with one of my friends or experimenting with hair color, Faye took pity on Gerald and took him with her, teaching him how to spot edible mushrooms in the woods or how to saddle a horse. It didn't matter to Gerald that we mostly just tolerated him. He liked being around people who didn't consider him a joke.

Gerald's family moved away that summer, and I always wondered how much of my influence stuck with him. At his new school, did he go back to doing crazy stunts to get noticed, or did he have a better sense of himself? At Allport no one much noticed his absence. Some of my friends spoke of my losing my little slave, but that wasn't how I thought of Gerald. I think if a person has…I guess *charm* is the right word, she should use it to help others become the best people they can be. That's what I tried to do with Gerald.

Bill was the same type of guy. He wanted to be important, wanted to be part of something. Ted had come along promising the moon, and Bill agreed to do what he asked without putting much thought into how serious the situation might become. Now he was involved in the murder of an FBI agent, and he was in big trouble. I'd have bet Bill didn't even know what the plan for the weekend was.

I decided to work on Bill the way I'd worked on Gerald, showing him his better side and offering an alternative to Ted's plotting. To get what she wants with men like Bill, a woman is sweet but a little aloof. The guy should doubt where he stands in her estimation, hoping for approval but unsure how to please her. I'd started getting Bill on my side by helping with the call from his boss. Now he felt he owed me something, which made him vulnerable.

There was no sense attempting to influence Ted. Guys like him never swerve from the path they've chosen, and they have no better nature to appeal to. Still, the fact that he'd called someone else for instructions when we blundered onto his murder scene meant he wasn't the big boss. I hoped the person above him wanted us alive, because I guessed Ted would have no qualms about killing again. My job for Saturday was to work around Ted while I used my carrot-and-stick allure on good old Bill.

Chapter Fourteen

Barb

I checked my phone a couple of times Friday evening, but there was nothing from Faye or Retta. I curled up on the sofa with a book, and Brat immediately jumped up to put herself between me and the pages. My cat doesn't approve of reading.

I moved the book to a spot where I could see it and gave her some of the squeezes along the backbone that she likes so well. In that position we reached an agreement. I could read as long as I didn't forget about her.

Living inside had softened the cat's fur, and having enough to eat had rounded out her shape. Her two trips to the vet (which were quite the experience) had resulted in treatment for ear mites and worms along with the usual shots. She'd responded well and been proclaimed generally healthy.

A low growl in the cat's throat signaled trouble, and I looked up from my book. Buddy stood at the top of the stairs, his homely face wrinkled in concern.

My first thought was to shoo him away. He'd never come up to my apartment before, and it was obvious my cat didn't want him there. A second later I asked myself why he was there. Certainly he missed Faye, but I doubted he thought she was hiding in my bedroom. Was he trying to tell me something?

He gave a single "Woof" that was neither loud nor aggressive. The Brat growled, but Buddy didn't react. After holding my gaze for a moment, he turned and went back downstairs.

He wanted me to know something, but I had no idea what it might be.

Chapter Fifteen

Faye

My mind roiled and rumbled all night, unable to stop thinking dark thoughts and imagining dire endings. At some point I must have slept, because when I opened my eyes, it was five a.m. Ted sat in the chair, and Bill lay sprawled on the floor with his head resting on his arms. His breathing was deep and regular, and I knew I'd missed my chance to escape the room. Ted seemed to read my mind and know I'd been plotting. A raised, mocking eyebrow told me he had the upper hand and knew it.

At seven he ordered me to get dressed for my day of retreat events. Retta was hostage to my good behavior, and he repeated that I should participate "—with a smile on your face."

Reluctantly, I showered and got dressed, half-listening to a discussion of breakfast. While I would be served a full meal in the dining room, Ted, Bill, and Retta would have to share one room service order.

"We can ask for extra," Bill proposed. "Say she has guests."

"Guests for breakfast?" Retta was horrified. "They'll either think I'm cheating the hotel or that I invited some man to spend the night."

"Oh, yeah," Bill agreed. "I guess that wouldn't look good."

Ted looked at him in disbelief. "Seriously? You're worried about the old girl's reputation?"

"If she's supposed to be in pain," I said from the bathroom, "why would she have guests?"

Reluctantly Ted accepted my argument. "Okay, the two of you share a breakfast." He took up Retta's purse, rummaged through it, and found her keys. "I'll take her car and find myself some breakfast."

"I guess I'm ready." I'd dressed in the Saturday outfit Retta planned for me, the only pair of zip-up pants I own (black, of course) with a turquoise top cut aslant at the waist. Black, low-heeled sandals completed the outfit—at least, I thought so. Jumping up from her seat on the bed, Retta adjusted the top so that it hung better on my shoulders. From a cloth bag she took a necklace and matching bracelet with oddly-shaped bits of metal set with turquoise and held it up.

"You forgot the accessories."

We were the victims of kidnapping murderers, and my sister still felt the need to fix me.

"This sets the outfit off," she said, fastening the necklace for me. "I'll bet someone asks where you bought it."

A glance at my reflection made me wince, because it looked like someone else standing there. I was supposed to go downstairs and act like the sort of woman who dressed this way every day, when all I really wanted to be doing on a weekend morning was heading out to the farm to see my sons, the kids, and the menagerie of animals they kept and loved as much as I did.

Retta examined me critically. "Put a little blush on, Sweetie. You're pale."

"I really—"

"You can't put on a great outfit and not do the makeup," she interrupted. Obediently I returned to the bathroom to apply blush. "And lipstick," she ordered. "There's a burgundy shade in my kit that will look nice on you."

"Is she always like that?" Ted asked when I'd done as she ordered. "Telling you what to do all the time?"

I didn't answer, but in the mirror I saw Ted point a finger at Retta as he spoke to Bill. "She's one of them people that's all sweetness and light while she pushes everybody around. Don't let her get away with it, understand?"

As I made my way downstairs, I thought Ted, though certainly not a nice person, was a pretty shrewd judge of character. It usually takes people much longer than a few hours to figure Retta out.

Breakfast was served buffet style. A woman at one station offered mimosas for the stout of heart, but I went on to the chafing dishes full of bacon, sausage, crepes, and hash browns. When my plate was full, I headed for a table. Not many were up this early, which might have been due to the poolside wine-tasting the night before. We'd heard them under our window, chatting and laughing until well past midnight.

Dina Engel stood waiting while a chef whipped up the omelet she'd requested. Stopping beside her I said, "Good morning." She returned my greeting, but she seemed distracted. I really wanted to know what was going on inside that head of hers.

"May I join you for breakfast?" I indicated the almost empty room. "I'm guessing some of the ladies had too much fun last night."

She seemed neither pleased nor displeased by my invitation, which brought out my insecurities. Was I too pushy? Had Dina taken an instant dislike to me? Did she prefer eating alone? Would she pretend to enjoy my company because she couldn't think of a way to refuse my offer?

Come to my home, and I'll feed you good food and talk all day, but don't set me down in a roomful of strangers and make me chat while I eat someone else's cooking.

Dina glanced at the doorway, where Angel was helping Rosalind Rayburn to a chair. "I'm supposed to sit with them, but—Thanks. I'll tell them I met an old friend and want to catch up."

When she'd spoken to Angel and gotten a seraphim-sized hug, Dina returned to the omelet table and picked up her plate. "They're very nice people, but I'm not sure I can handle another discussion of clever ways to prepare tart cherries right now."

"I don't promise sparkling conversation," I warned. It was nice to be chosen as the better of two choices, though I did have a moment of regret for the recipes I was missing out on. I love cherry anything.

We chose an empty table and sat, taking a few moments to locate sugar for our coffee and butter for the toast from the selections at its center. Dina ate as if she didn't taste her food at all, and I began to doubt myself again. What should a small-town woman with barely two nickels to rub together talk about to someone whose background was cosmopolitan—and criminal?

Probably realizing the silence had lengthened between us Dina said, "Where are you from?"

Mention of Allport brought a vague look, so I located it Michigan style, by pointing to the top joint of the index finger on my hand. She nodded vaguely, as people from the Detroit area tend to do when you admit you live "up north." For many of them it's like a foreign land.

Detecting little interest on her part in what Allport is like, I turned the conversation to what was probably her favorite topic. "You're launching a clothing line at—what are you, thirty? Thirty-two?" Flattery is always good.

She smiled. "I'm a little past that, but yes. It took me till almost forty to decide to do what I've always wanted to do."

"I know exactly what you mean." Creating the Smart Detective Agency had been my idea, though I'd never have had the nerve to do it without Barb. Of course I didn't tell Dina I was on the side of law and order, in case she wasn't. "We don't all move at the same pace, and that's okay. After your show tomorrow, you'll be on your way."

"I hope so." Her brow furrowed. It was plain to me that something had happened between last night and this morning that shifted her mild apprehension about the show to real worry.

"Is there a problem?"

Her grimace might have signaled anger. "Depends who you ask."

"What went wrong?"

She shook her head as if to say she couldn't explain, but her lips moved involuntarily. Dina had no reason to talk about her troubles to a stranger, but she wanted badly to tell someone.

Barb and Retta say I have a sense about people. That might or might not be true, but I do listen with my feelings and not just with my mind. I think it comes from my not wanting to "fix" people, the way my sisters do. They don't mean to tell you what you should do, but honestly, they both do it.

Dina Engel felt betrayed, and she was having trouble keeping it to herself. I knew I couldn't remedy whatever was wrong, but I thought it would help if she just told someone about it. But how did I let her know it was okay to share?

A little confidential disclosure might help. "Listen," I said. "I'm kind of here under false pretenses."

She looked surprised. "What do you mean?"

With a gesture that took in the whole area I confessed, "It was my sister who really wanted to do this Love-Able Ladies thing. Now she's laid up in our room with a bad back, and I'm floating around with nothing to do. If you want to talk, I'll listen for as long as it takes, and I won't tell anyone what you say." I wriggled my brows. "I might if they pull out my fingernails, but otherwise I'm good at keeping secrets."

She smiled at my joke then sobered again. "It's Roger—my father." The last word came out like a curse. "It's like he's determined to mess this up for me."

For all her forty years, Dina Engel sounded exactly like a dozen teenagers who'd sat at my kitchen table over the years and said similar things about one parent or the other. However, I had a feeling that this time it was more than Dear Old Dad wearing socks with sandals or refusing to buy that classic Chevelle as a Sweet 16 birthday gift.

"What did he do?"

She pressed her lips together, fighting to keep her complaint inside, but in the end it didn't work. "My mom died a year ago, after almost a decade of illness. I'd taken care of her all that time, and with her gone, I needed something to do with the rest of my life. I asked Roger for the money to start a business." She glared at the salt shaker for a moment. "He owed me. I did it for her, but he—He owed me."

Money is often a problem between parents and children, but calling her father *Roger* while her mother was *Mom* was telling. "You asked your father to help you get started as a designer?"

She nodded. "We've never been close, but Roger's got plenty of money. It was no burden for him to give me a stake to get started."

Parents often feel differently about that than children do, but I said, "He agreed to help when you explained how much it meant to you?"

She made a helpless gesture. "Roger doesn't let you explain anything, and he certainly didn't care how I felt. He agreed to fund my project, but there were strings attached. I got a line of credit and two years to turn a profit. After that, I have to start paying him back." Looking down at her plate she said, "I wanted it so badly, you know? I wanted to feel like my life wasn't a total waste, like my—" She chewed on her lip. "—like people who never try."

Like her mother, from what I'd read. A life lived in the shadow of a controlling husband.

While Engel's deal didn't seem like something a doting father would offer, it wasn't unreasonable, so there had to be more. "You got the chance to make Detroit Chic successful. What's gone wrong?"

Dina pushed her plate away and patted her lips with her napkin. "Roger insisted I have a financial overseer." Her lips tightened. "He tried to make it sound like it was a benefit but really, he wants control."

"When you're just starting out—" I began, but she interrupted.

"I know the fashion business: fabric, weave, chemistry, dyes, materials used for buttons, belts, and accessories—I studied all that."

She sipped at her tea. "People think it's all just drawing pictures of skirts and dresses, but there's a lot more to it."

"Most jobs seem easier to outsiders than they actually are," I said.

"I took classes in finance too. I have a four-year business degree."

Which didn't mean she could manage both ends of the business in today's complex climate. Her father might know her weaknesses better than Dina was willing to admit. "Maybe he wanted to let you concentrate on the artistic part of things."

She made a sarcastic *pfft*. "You don't know Roger."

I gave up trying to defend a parent's tendency toward caution. "Well, at least you've got a start. Are things going well?"

"They were." She stirred more sugar into her tea. "But Roger took it upon himself to reduce my expenses for the show this weekend—without the courtesy of letting me know."

"What do you mean?"

Dina set her cup in its saucer. "Do you know who Roger Engel is?"

I managed a confused look to indicate I was thinking but couldn't come up with anything concrete. It was better than an outright lie.

"He runs several night clubs in the Detroit area." When I nodded noncommittally, she went on. "His money-saving idea for me was to cancel the contract I'd arranged with a reputable agency and send a group of his dancers to act as models for my show."

"Oh." That didn't sound like caution. It sounded like disaster.

She ran her hand through her light-colored hair, pulling it up and off her neck then dropping it back into place. "My designs are classy, and the women at this retreat stand for female dignity and old-fashioned values. The models tomorrow morning will be ten exotic dancers who wouldn't know class if it crawled up on the stage and slapped them."

"Oh." I really couldn't think of anything else to say.

"Besides that, they've no doubt altered themselves in all kinds of wild ways in order to be different and recognizable."

"You mean—?"

"Right. Boob jobs, tats, piercings—the whole gamut." She did the hair thing again. "Not only that, but my clothes are sized for mature women. They won't even fit right."

"Wow." At least it wasn't another *Oh.*

Dina toyed with a chunk of melon she'd left on her plate. "I suppose I could turn on some funk and let them show the Love-Able Ladies why men flock to Roger's clubs when their wives aren't looking."

I suppressed an involuntary smile at the mental image of club dancers grinding their way through the horrified crowd. "I can't imagine that would go over well. What will you do?"

"Something—I just don't know what yet." Her brows met as she made a decision. "I have a rehearsal scheduled for this afternoon. If I can make the clothes fit and teach the girls some basic fashion modelling, I'll go ahead with it."

"Those are two big ifs."

"Yup." She shook her head. "Wish I could be in three places at once."

The thought that popped into my head scared me, but at the same time it was a heaven-sent opportunity. Someone had a crime planned during Dina's show. If I were inside her circle, I might find out who it was and what was going to happen.

Without thinking it through as much as I probably should have, I offered, "I could do fittings while you oversee the rehearsal. If I take notes on what needs to be done, you can make the alterations afterward."

"You know how to do that?"

Alterations were once my specialty, though I never admitted it outside my own home. Since money was always tight and boys grow like weeds, I used to buy the nicest men's garments I could find at second-hand stores and fit them to my sons by taking them apart and reassembling them. I can't say I enjoyed it, but I know how to re-set a sleeve, take in or let out a dart, and re-size pants completely by separating the front from the back, adjusting the fit, and putting them back together. It was a source of pride for me that no one but us knew my family's dress clothes were never new.

"I told you this retreat wasn't my idea" I reminded Dina. "As long as I'm here, I might as well help if I can."

"What if your sister feels better tomorrow?"

The thought of Retta's situation made me hesitate, but I'd been ordered to be visible at the events, and I would be. "When her back goes," I replied, "it's usually a day before her pain meds kick in. I can give you the whole afternoon."

Dina's spine straightened a little. "The models are due to arrive around twelve. I told Honny to bring them in through the kitchen."

"Honny?" It sounded like *honey* but I noticed the spelling later in the program.

"The watchdog my father assigned to me. He's driving up with the clothes and the 'models.'" She rolled her eyes. "I'm not expecting ten Heidi Klums."

"Where will the rehearsal be?"

"Here." She took her phone and notebook from the chair beside her. "We have the room from one till four. Then they have to set up for dinner."

"I'll find you after lunch then."

I left feeling sorry for Dina. The stress of launching a business was bad enough, but to have its success threatened by her father's interference—and stinginess—made things ten times worse. Once I'd walked away, I cautioned myself to remain objective. A detective can't just take what someone tells her at face value. Dina might be seeing things from a skewed perspective. Or she might be lying for some reason, though I couldn't think of one that fit the circumstances.

Should I have warned her she might be in danger? I wasn't sure she was. If she was part of Roger Engel's schemes, Dina might already be aware that an FBI agent had been murdered. She might have had breakfast with me to see if I'd tell the first sympathetic person I met that my sister was a prisoner and I was a hostage.

Still, she'd seemed one hundred percent focused on launching her business. Could she be so convincingly distressed if the event was merely a cover-up for some impending crime?

Confused and uncertain, I put the decision off. Instead I made the choice to attend the morning session titled Romantic Vacation Cruises rather than Coping techniques for Widows. At least in the former there would be pretty pictures.

Chapter Sixteen

Barb

On Saturday morning I was surprised to find no messages from either sister. For Faye, that wasn't unusual. Having gone from hating her smart phone to merely being irritated by it, she might have turned it off to enjoy the conference. But Retta? No way. The woman walked around with her cell in one hand, as if letting go would end the world as we know it. For her to miss a message and a voice mail was highly unusual.

After trying to call both of them and getting no answer, I called the inn's front desk. A pleasant young man told me my sisters had checked in Friday. He just as pleasantly connected me to the land line in their room, which rang and rang. No one answered. "They're probably involved in some activity," he said when I called back. He added in a tone of amusement, "There are Love-Able Ladies all over the place." In a more helpful vein he offered to page one of them but advised waiting until the sessions broke for lunch. "Unless it's an emergency," he said diffidently.

Was it an emergency? I couldn't say it was, since I knew my sisters had arrived safely. If Faye had had a heart attack or Retta had slipped on her too-tall, spiky heels and broken an ankle, this guy would know about it. They had to be okay.

But it didn't feel right. I went out to the shed, where Dale was already at work. Buddy lay just inside the door, tacitly proclaiming that if Faye wasn't nearby, he considered Dale second-best. "You still haven't heard from Faye?"

"No." He rubbed the back of his neck with a weather-beaten, work-roughened hand.

"The inn people don't know of any problems, but I just called their cells again and got no answer. Do you think I should be worried?"

He gave me a rueful smile. "I was trying not to worry myself."

"It isn't like them to stay quiet this long."

Dale applied a wrench to a bolt. "Can you call that FBI agent they're working with?"

"Good idea." But Auburn's phone went directly to voicemail, where a recording asked me to leave a message and promised he'd get back to me. I asked him to return my call as soon as possible.

Dale spoke, almost to himself. "These are the times when I feel the most useless."

A falling tree branch—often called a widow-maker—and the resulting head trauma had left Dale able to drive only short distances and preferably to familiar places. Noise, movement, and light distracted and disoriented him, making longer trips uncomfortable and dangerous. "If you'll keep an eye on the office," I said glancing at my watch, "I'll head over there and check on them."

I should never have let them go without me.

Less than an hour later I was on the road with a small bag in case I stayed overnight. Telling myself I was over-reacting didn't help, and Dale had been openly relieved by my decision. Subsequent calls to Auburn's phone netted no result, and the receptionist at the Bureau in Detroit could only tell me that the agent was currently unavailable. Though I wasn't ready to tell the FBI there was an emergency, I felt in my gut that there was.

GPS took me to St. Millicent's, but it was a slow trip. Traffic was summer weekend heavy, and the mostly two-lane roads didn't allow many places for passing. It was noon by the time I reached the inn, and the desk clerk informed me the retreat guests had just gone in to lunch. There was a speaker, so they wouldn't come out again until after one.

I asked if there'd been any trouble, but she shook her head. "They seem to be having a good time." Leaning toward me a little she said, "I bet a few are hung over from the wine-tasting at the pool last night."

My sisters were unlikely candidates for that affliction. Retta can hold her liquor, and Faye seldom drinks at all. If she'd over-indulged in an attempt to fit in, she might be too sick to call, but—No. That didn't sound like Faye at all, nor did it explain why Retta hadn't returned calls and messages.

As I expected, hotel policy prevented the clerk from telling me which room was theirs. I located the dining room, but a woman outside the closed doors told me politely but firmly that no one without a retreat badge was admitted inside. I'd have to wait until the meal and the speaker were finished in order to see if my sisters were in there.

Now should I claim an emergency? The serene atmosphere suggested no such thing. Aside from the hum of conversation and the clink of silverware inside the room, the inn was silent. I looked at my watch. Forty minutes, maybe less. I would wait.

Chapter Seventeen

Retta

My dislike for Ted didn't get any better on Saturday morning. After deciding Bill and I would share one breakfast, he rummaged through my purse and took my keys, claiming he'd find a place to eat somewhere off the property. Bill was slightly apologetic, explaining that Ted had no vehicle of his own. "He came with his girlfriend," he said, "and she's staying down the road somewhere."

"Shut up," Ted ordered. "They don't need to know nothing."

Before Ted left, he and Bill stood near the door for a few minutes, speaking in low tones. Bill was agitated; Ted was placating, but in a commanding, superior way. Whatever he said shut Bill up, at least temporarily.

While they talked, I ordered breakfast. When I heard the door close, I looked up to see that Ted was gone. Bill seemed put out that I hadn't ask for his input, but I explained it should appear to be my order, not his. In a few minutes a girl brought the meal on a tray and I did my bad-back routine again. When Bill emerged from his hiding place in the bathroom, he took the cover off the main dish, bent over to glare at it, and announced he hated green peppers in an omelet. "You can have it," he said grumpily. "I'll eat the toast."

"I always have toast with an omelet," I told him. "We'll split it."

It turned out Bill didn't care for raisin bread either. His expression got even grumpier as he picked the dark, chewy morsels out with the knife and dumped them onto a napkin as if they were fried June bugs. Finished with that, he spread the tattered remains with jam, filling in the holes with determined precision. Feeling a little sorry for him I offered the orange juice, but apparently citric acid doesn't go well with grape jam and a nervous stomach. Bill turned up his nose at half the coffee too, since I'd already added cream and sugar.

Between bites of the omelet (which was deliciously fluffy), I asked, "How did you get hooked up with Ted? You don't seem like the criminal type."

Bill frowned as if he'd asked himself the same thing. "This place doesn't pay so great, you know?" He looked embarrassed. "Ted offered me a lot of money if I let him stay in my room over the garage and keep my mouth shut about it."

"No one's supposed to know he's around?"

"I thought him and his girl was gonna rob the rooms or maybe the guests' cars." His gaze dropped to the floor. "No way I thought anybody'd get hurt."

"Murdered." I said it softly, not an accusation, but a reminder.

Bill raised his hands, palms out. "He says the guy attacked him."

"From inside his car? And Ted just happened to be carrying both a gun and a knife on his person?"

Bill lowered his head like a stubborn bull. "He had to do it."

"You didn't actually see what happened when the guy got killed."

"No, I was out in the vineyard. Ted came and found me so I could help him get the—so I could help him. When we got to the parking lot, there you two were, looking right into the car." In a justification typical of criminals everywhere he added, "If you'd just stayed away, things woulda been all right."

"Bill, that man was an FBI agent. When it's discovered he's missing, there will be a response like you can't believe."

"That's why we had to get rid of the—the evidence. By the time they find out he's—not around anymore, we'll be long gone."

"You're leaving with Ted when this is over?"

He took a long drink from the glass of the water he'd got from the bathroom sink. "He says I can work for his boss and make a sh—lots of money."

"Are you sure you can trust him?"

"I'll be okay." Gathering the remains of our meal on the tray, he checked the hallway to be sure it was empty then set it outside the door. When he returned he said, "You ladies will be okay too. Ted says we got no reason to hurt you."

And if you believe that, I've got some snake oil right here.

We settled in to watch the morning shows on TV. As insipid hosts mugged and emoted, I tried to plan my future—*any* future. I could keep trying to win Bill over, maybe get him to release me, but it was pretty clear he was afraid of Ted. I heard it in his voice when he spoke of the man. I eyed the door, wondering if I could get to it and call for help, but Bill had set the intruder bar, which would slow me down. In addition, Ted had ordered him to stay between me and the door at all times, and he hadn't forgotten once. If I started screaming for help, would Bill have the nerve to—

Static sounded, and Bill took the radio from his belt. "Yeah?"

"Where are you?" a female voice asked.

He looked at me with confusion in his eyes. "I'm—uh—a guest is having trouble with her—uh—"

I pointed to the latch on my suitcase.

"—her luggage. It won't open."

"Well, when you're finished there, Jerry needs help setting up."

Bill rolled his eyes. "I can't. I gotta—" He stalled again, and I made sawing gestures. "Oh, right! I gotta do some trimming out back. Greg said he wants it done today, so you'll have to get someone else for the inside stuff."

"Okay." The woman sounded doubtful, and why wouldn't she? They had over a hundred guests and their maintenance man insisted he was busy elsewhere.

Bill replaced the radio in its holster. "Thanks. I have trouble when I gotta think fast."

"Lots of us need a few seconds to process," I said. "It doesn't mean you're not smart."

He huffed a negative. "That's not what most people say."

"Well, most people are wrong then." Bill almost smiled before he remembered I was his prisoner and he was supposed to be stern.

A few minutes later a click at the door signaled Ted's entry. He looked satisfied and smelled faintly of bacon. As the scent wafted toward us, Bill's gloomy expression hinted regret at his own skimpy breakfast.

Ted made a startling announcement. "We're taking her out of here."

"Why?" I demanded.

"None of your business." He turned to Bill. "You said there was an old shed on the property with a door that locks?"

"A chain with a padlock."

"Have you got the key?"

Bill shrugged. "They just hang it under the eaves. It ain't like anybody's going to go looking for it."

"Are there windows she could crawl out of?"

"There's one, but it's boarded up."

"Good. She can spend the rest of the weekend there, and you can show up for work so nobody goes looking for you."

Bill frowned. "It's gonna be hot today. That closed-up place will be like an oven."

"If it bothers you," Ted said grimly, "I can take care of her like I did the FBI guy."

With a gasp worthy of a soap opera Bill said, "You told me you weren't gonna hurt her."

"Yeah." Ted didn't sound pleased. "But you're supposed to be working, and I got stuff to do. We need to put her somewhere we can keep her secure." He turned to me. "You'll be fine if you behave yourself, but don't get cute. If I have to, I'll kill you in a heartbeat and then do the same for your sister."

I thought about promising to behave if they left me here in the room, but I knew that wouldn't fly. Faye would be horrified when she returned to find me gone, but the move might be good. Without someone guarding me, I might find a way to get free.

It never hurts to be optimistic.

Ted didn't let me bring anything, not even a lipstick. Gripping my arm, he guided me while Bill went ahead as a scout, stopping at corridor intersections and peering through the outside doors before we exited. His behavior was almost comically suspicious, but since the staff was busy and the guests were closed in their sessions, the only person we saw was a maid whose trim rear was toward us as she vacuumed the hallway.

At the south entry door we stepped into blinding sunlight and a rush of air even warmer than the day before. By mid-afternoon the heat would indeed be unbearable. "This way," Bill called softly, and we walked across the lawn and down the edge of the parking lot. Seen from the inn we might have been a couple led by an inn employee to some spot we'd asked directions to.

The trees that flanked the vineyard on the north and south were mostly maple and oak with a few pines mixed in. Turning south, Bill followed a path the forest had almost reclaimed. Low-hanging branches impeded our progress, and a few downed saplings required us to either duck or step over their dying trunks. Once we were away from the inn Bill said, "I'm supposed to be clearing this to make a cross-country ski trail for next winter."

I let a drooping branch go and barely missed whacking Ted in the face. When he swore I turned with an innocent expression. "Sorry!"

"Keep going," he growled, "or some skier will find your bones on the trail come February."

When we reached the shed, my optimism faded. I'd pictured a slanted wooden structure with rotting boards, but my new prison was made of cement blocks set on a concrete slab. I wouldn't be bashing a hole in a wall or digging out from under it, even if there were any tools inside. Bill retrieved the key, unlocked the padlock, and opened the wide, double doors. The place was empty except some low piles of metal junk and a vintage tractor, the kind with a hole in the front for a crank that started the engine.

A shove at my back sent me staggering forward, and the doors closed behind me, shutting out almost all the light. "Lock it up tight," I heard Ted order. "Then go back and let them see you at the inn. We don't want anybody wondering where you went to."

Bill's attempt at reassurance came through the crack between the doors. "It's been empty for years," he said in a low voice. "I don't think there's any big critters living in there, just bugs and that."

That wasn't reassuring. It was also dark and stifling, about ninety degrees.

Hurrying to the door I spoke softly, hoping Ted had already gone. "Will you bring me some water, Bill?"

There was a long pause, and his reply was almost inaudible. "I can't—"

"You're not the kind of person who'd leave me here to die of the heat, are you?"

His voice got even softer. "I'll try."

I gave him my best smile, though he couldn't see it. They say a smile reflects in a person's voice. "You're a good man."

There was a click as the padlock engaged, fastening the chain that held the doors closed. I thought I heard a tap, as if he'd patted the door once in regret. Then all was silent.

Chapter Eighteen

Faye

Like a stream of obedient lambs, we trooped into the dining room after the morning session. Some of the women stopped to peruse the vendors' wares, and I noticed the same bored-looking girl at the perfume table. Today she wore a high-necked, long-sleeved pullover, despite the August weather. Covering tattoos, perhaps? As Dina said, most Love-Able Ladies wouldn't approve of body art, especially if it happened to be skulls, blood drops, or impolite suggestions.

Inside the dining room I looked for Dina in the crowd of women jockeying for chairs at the tables of their choice. She was nowhere in sight.

Throughout the morning I'd considered how I might tell her that an FBI agent had been murdered and the crime probably had something to do with her. It might create problems, because if she believed she was in danger, Dina might do something that put Retta at risk. Since whatever was going to happen was scheduled during the fashion show on Sunday morning, I figured I had time to decide on a course of action. At the moment my choice was to observe and not report.

I'd considered going up to our room to check on Retta, but there was really no reason to. I thought Bill and Ted would hold up their end of the bargain as long as I did my part. Surveying the women around me, I wondered again who the mysterious third person, my watcher, might be. It could be anyone, even Dina herself.

Joining a group of women, I listened to their chatter as waiters served ahi tuna with jicama slaw and crusty bread. The wines offered were Pinot Noir and Sangiovese. I ordered what the woman next to me took, since it was hard to care what I ate or drank. My companions seemed to have bonded in some way I didn't understand, so they pretty much ignored me. That was okay. I had a lot to think about.

The speaker for the noon meal was a humorist, and if all else had been well, I'd have enjoyed her stories of raising kids on one income to give them a "traditional" home life. After the audience howled with laughter at her monologue about leaving the baby at church after services one Sunday, she ended with the theme of her message: She'd chosen to be a full-time mother because it was what was best for her family. The women around me met each other's eyes and nodded agreement.

Barb would have reminded them that women have always worked, whether in the fields, in the home, or at the family business. The Ozzie-and-Harriet-type family, where Dad goes to work and Mom stays home and bakes cookies, is a nice arrangement for some. Barb would insist, and I'd have to agree with her, that there's room in the world for other models.

That's why I always end up in the middle on important questions. I don't mind a lot of things feminists despise, like pink for girls and blue for boys. Most people are comfortable when they know their role in the world. When roles interfere with an individual's choices, then they need to be examined. My approach is pretty practical. Use the roles that work for you; ignore the ones that don't.

A waiter came through the kitchen doorway, and I caught a glimpse of Dina Engel inside. Though she was turned away from me, tension radiated from her like the glow of a lightsaber. Excusing myself with a smile, I left the speaker summing up and went to see what new crisis Dina was dealing with. As I stepped into the kitchen I heard her speaking to someone I couldn't see. Her voice sounded harsh. "If she's going to be a problem, I want you to get rid of her," she said coldly. "I don't want anything else to go wrong."

Backing away, I turned to a table set with desserts and pretended to consider my choice. Who was the problem person who'd made Dina so angry, the one she wanted to be rid of? Suddenly it was imperative that I go upstairs and make sure Retta was safe.

Chapter Nineteen

Barb

I circled the common area outside the inn's dining room, waiting for my sisters to finish lunch. Vendor tables set in arcs offered products and services of interest to women—at least some women. I stayed away from the fragrance table, though a young woman with lanky hair and too much eye makeup eyed me hopefully. Perfume makes me sneeze, and I suspected if I went anywhere near her, she'd spritz me. When I moved in the opposite direction she took up her phone and began scrolling, her hair falling forward like a curtain between us.

There was a table of exotic teas, loose-leaf, of course, and an array of books by a woman whose name I recognized as a successful romance novelist from the '60s. She had to be in her nineties, but I supposed her publisher trotted her out at events like this to keep the inventory moving. A poster on an easel invited attendees to write their goals for the retreat. *Become more feminine-G.S.* was scribbled next to a neatly printed: *Find a diet that works for me-Dora.*

The Bellarina shoes table stood next to one filled with purses whose price tags made me shake my head in disgust. Farther down was a small tent that offered personalized, private fittings of "foundation garments"—very expensive ones.

Another table had registration forms for future Love-Able Ladies Retreats, and scanning the details, I was shocked at the cost. We hadn't paid, of course, but it was hard for me to understand why anyone would fork over that much money to be brainwashed. The next table was a sign-up for the in-house spa, and the surface was peppered with little star-shaped signs that offered what someone considered encouragement:

Don't worry your pretty little head—Take it to the girls at our salon!

We can teach you exercises that will make your man say, "Nice butt!"

Smile! Our tooth-whitening treatments will make him eager for more!

The last one was too much. I have what is sometimes referred to as RBF, a face that in repose looks angry and forbidding. I blame it on my astigmatism, which makes me frown in order to focus. Over the years, male colleagues thought it was ever-so-witty to tell me to "Smile!" when we met in the corridor or crossed paths in the parking lot. Who greets professional men with cutesy commands like that?

Since my retirement I'd begun anonymously correcting public mistakes in grammar, punctuation, and usage, whether it was badly-composed signs, television personalities with poor grammar skills, or newspapers too cheap to hire competent editors. The only person aware of it was Retta, who'd found out by accident and held it over my head ever since. While I didn't think she'd ever tell on me, I hadn't had the nerve to test her on it yet.

None of the signs before me had grammatical errors, but I felt an overwhelming need to draw attention to their blatant sexism. Forcing women into boxes is bad enough when men do it, but why would women encourage other women to think they only matter if they have pretty heads, nice butts, and oh-so-white teeth?

Taking a blank sign-up sheet and a convenient ink pen, I turned the paper over and wrote in block letters on the back: *I see my body as an instrument rather than an ornament. ~Alanis Morissette.* Folding the sheet in half, I set it like a tent in the middle of the table.

Pleased with that, I returned to the poster of goals and wrote in one corner, *The emotional, sexual, and psychological stereotyping of females begins when the doctor says, "It's a girl." ~Shirley Chisholm*

When I turned, the woman at the perfume table was looking at me. I managed a semi-casual smile, and she returned to whatever she was doing on her phone. Wandering to a corner where there was a bench, I sat down and read a book on my phone until I heard applause and a shifting of chairs. The doors of the dining room opened, and women streamed out, chatting and laughing.

I didn't see my sisters in the first few groups, but finally I spotted Faye exiting alone. Relieved to see she was okay, I waved. She seemed for a moment to have seen me, but she didn't respond. Turning sharply left, she went into the bathroom. That I understood, as many women over fifty do. I'd already been there myself.

When Faye didn't come out after several minutes, I went in to see what was taking so long. The rest room was one of those two-entry setups, with a small vestibule that had no purpose I could see and a second door leading to the stalls, sinks, and mirrors. Faye wasn't in the vestibule, so I went on to where a line of women waited for a turn in one of three stalls. Two stood at the sinks, washing their hands while peering at their reflections. Faye stood behind them, brushing her hair with her fingers. That in itself was unusual, since she tends to comb it once in the morning and ignore it for the rest of the day. Catching my eye in the mirror, she telegraphed a warning not to speak until we were alone.

I stood off to one side as if waiting to use a stall. In the few minutes it took for the others to finish up and leave, my mind bubbled with questions. "Where is Retta?" was foremost among them, so when we were alone I asked that first.

"She's in our room." Faye seemed unable to decide where to begin explaining.

"When neither of you answered our calls and messages, I drove over. What's going on?"

The story came then: the murder of Agent Auburn, their discovery of the corpse before the killers could dispose of it, their capture, and the holding of Retta as a hostage.

"What are these men up to?"

Faye shrugged. "All I know is they need the retreat to continue without incident."

"Why?"

"I guess so Dina Engel gets to do her show."

"And that matters why?"

Faye showed a rare burst of anger. "I've been trying to find that out, Barb." She was scared.

I put a hand on her arm. "I'm here now, Faye. We can fix this."

Calming, she explained she'd volunteered to help at the rehearsal that would be starting soon. "I thought if I get to know Dina, I can decide if she's *in* danger or if she *is* the danger."

"I get it. She should be warned, but then what happens to Retta?"

Faye sighed. "The men claim they'll let us go once whatever is supposed to happen is over."

"And you believe that?"

I got a look I seldom got from my sister—well, this sister. "I wasn't born yesterday, Barb. They killed an FBI agent, so why not a couple of middle-aged women? It's why I've been careful to do as they said."

We had to call the police, but Faye was right—first we had to consider the consequences. This far from the city, I guessed it would take a while for law enforcement to organize a rescue. That meant Faye had to continue to play her part while I assessed the situation. She would be compliant, and I would give the police specifics about what was needed when I called for help. "You say there are two men you know about?"

She nodded. "Ted is mean as a snake, and Bill is…susceptible to Retta. She's already working on softening him up."

Retta could sell mittens in Tahiti if men were doing the shopping. "Might he let her go?"

Faye shook her head. "He'll do little things for her, but he's too afraid of Ted to do more."

I sighed. "Okay. Describe them for me."

"Bill is about our age and average-looking except he has a streak of silver at the front of his hair. Ted is younger, tough-looking, and blond." She frowned. "They said there's a third person who's watching to see that I keep quiet. That's why I didn't speak when I first saw you." She shifted her feet. "It's also why we can't stay in here. They'll wonder why I'm taking so long."

"Right."

"Barb, what if they hurt Retta?"

"As long as she's their means of making you behave, she's safe." I hoped I was telling the truth. "Give me your room key, and I'll check to make sure she's okay."

She dug it out and handed it over. "How will you do it?"

"I'll pretend to be the manager. I heard we have a sick guest, and I'm concerned."

"After that are you going to call the police?"

"We have to." She frowned, but she knew I was right. "Until they get here, let these people think they've got you under their control."

We moved to the vestibule, where a large, fifty-ish woman was just sitting down on a padded chair in the corner. Taking off one shoe, she rubbed her foot. When she moved her head, I noticed an odd effect: her hair was purple under a black top layer. I wondered for a moment how someone did that—and why. It was beyond my comprehension. I also noticed a butterfly tattooed on her upper thigh and smiled to myself. Even Love-Able Ladies must sometimes feel the tug of popular culture.

"Not used to wearing heels anymore," she commented as we passed.

"I hear you," Faye replied. "I'm missing my tennies too."

Outside the rest room we parted as casual strangers, Faye heading for Dina's rehearsal while I went to see what I could do about freeing our captive sister.

Except she wasn't there. I knocked on the door of Room 210, ignoring the *Do Not Disturb* card hung over the handle. "It's the manager, ma'am." I waited, but there was no answer. I tried again. "Management."

Nothing. Pressing my ear to the door, I heard no sounds inside the room. After a third knock, I used Faye's key and stepped inside.

Retta's suitcase lay open on a folding stand. Faye's was on the floor in the far corner. Items scattered around the room testified to occupancy, but Retta and her captor were gone. Beside the TV was a sheet of hotel stationery with four words written in block print: *YOU KNOW THE DEAL.*

Chapter Twenty

Retta

It took a while for my eyes to adjust to the darkness in the shed. After a few minutes I could see that the place was about ten by fifteen feet, with a wooden roof supported by rough beams. A block and tackle overhead hinted at its use for machine repair at some time in the past. As Bill had said, the single window was boarded over, perhaps because two of its four glass panes were broken. Slits of sunlight showed between, but the boards themselves were solid when I reached through a shattered pane and tested them.

I tried pushing at the doors, hoping there'd be enough give between them that a petite woman could slide through. They gapped maybe two inches before the chain caught and held. I tried all four corners in the hope a hinge was loose or rotted. No luck.

Next I did a circuit of the place, touching the walls with my hands to keep from tripping over unseen items on the floor. Each time my foot hit something I stooped, hoping to find a tool useful for escape. I found only old tractor parts, at least that's what I judged them to be from the odd shapes and the heavy layers of grease. Not only were they useless, I had nowhere to wipe the gunk off my hands except the scratchy cement walls.

The air inside the shed was stale, hung with dust, and hot yet slightly clammy. The surrounding woods was deadly quiet. I could scream for help, but I guessed the only people anywhere near were Ted and Bill. Ted had made it clear: if I made trouble, I was expendable.

After my fruitless exploration of the walls, I turned my attention to the tractor, more visible as my eyes adjusted to the gloom. Even without being able to read the logo, I recognized its lines and familiar red paint. Dad had always had a Farmall, and most of his equipment was old, since our farm had been a bare-bones, single-family operation. This tractor was probably from the 1940s, which was both good and bad. According to Dad, older tractors are pretty simple machines that last forever if they're well-maintained. I had no idea if this one had been taken care of, but the fact that it was stored in a shed was a hopeful sign. Would they protect a piece of junk from the elements?

The front tires were small and close together. The back tires were almost my height and fat, with deep tread to push them through all kinds of terrain. Metal fenders shielded the driver from flying dirt (or manure). I recalled riding with Dad when I was little, him in the metal seat and me beside him, leaning against a fender and holding onto its edges with both hands. Today they'd cite a parent who let his kid ride that way for child endangerment, but in those days it was perfectly acceptable.

As I walked around the big machine, trying to recall what was what, Dad began singing songs in my mind. He'd always had a tune as he worked: whistled, hummed, or sung in syllables of "Dee-dee-dee." I suppose it meant he was a contented man, and the memory calmed me a little.

Climbing onto the tractor seat, I studied what was there. There was a single gauge on the dashboard, but I couldn't make out its purpose. Gas? Temperature? Oil pressure? It had been a long time since I'd had reason to pay attention.

Dad taught me to drive the tractor at a young age so I could pull the wagon while everyone else picked stone. He'd often joked the crop that grew best in Michigan was rocks. Each spring, new ones appeared in the fields and had to be toted to piles outside the ground to be planted. Mom, Barb, and Faye wrestled smaller stones onto the trailer while Dad handled the larger specimens. It was hot, back-breaking work that no one looked forward to. After Barb and Faye left home, Dad started hiring neighborhood boys to help him. I don't think Barbara Ann ever got over Dad "spoiling" me by hiring workers to do "my" job.

Back to the present and this particular tractor. Could I go back decades and remember how to start the thing? Three metal pedals were positioned in front of the driver's seat. I knew one was the brake and one the clutch. What was the other? I hoped I didn't need to know. There was a throttle on the steering column, a piece of fan-shaped metal with teeth along the top edge. A lever that moved along those teeth would control my speed if I got the engine started. The gearshift was on the left, and I took hold of the hard-rubber handle and wiggled it, practicing the different positions. Neutral, a sloppy area in the middle, was where the shifter had to be when the tractor started. If not, the person at the front with the crank—me, in this case—might get run over.

Even if I got the settings right, I still had to muster the strength to turn the crank, which, given the age of the machine, might be difficult. Dad had sometimes had trouble turning hard enough to start an engine, and he'd warned the crank could kick back, wrenching a shoulder or even breaking an arm.

I experimented for probably half an hour, but I couldn't remember the process. I tried setting the throttle low, then high, then in the middle. Each time I went to the front and turned the crank, but nothing happened. With a sore shoulder and a defeated attitude, I leaned against a rear tire, trying to come up with something else to try. Escape was essential, and all it took was remembering what had once been a normal task. Dad would have been disappointed in me, as I was in myself.

After a few minutes of sulking, I figured out that if the tractor couldn't get me out of there, at least it could raise me high enough to test the solidity of the shed roof. Standing on the seat, I could just reach the main support beam overhead. I wrapped my arms around it and hung there for a moment like a sloth on a tree branch. Dust and grime fell onto my face and hair as I pulled my bottom half up onto the beam, first one foot, then the other, then my torso, until I could twist myself and balance on hands and knees along its six-inch span. Slowly I made my way along it until I touched the rafters. Grasping one on either side of me, I stood up. To my great disappointment, every board within reach was firmly fastened in place. Worse, I found a knothole that revealed there was galvanized tin over the boards. There was no chance I could push my way out through the roof.

Lowering my rear to the beam I slid off, holding on for a second before dropping to the floor. My feet stung when I hit the concrete, and for a second I envied Faye her sensible, crepe-soled shoes.

Able to think of nothing more to do, I moved some spiders and their conquests out of the way with my foot and slumped into the corner they'd inhabited. Pulling my knees up, I laid my arms across them and rested my head on my arms. Where skin touched skin, I felt the grit that now coated my whole body. Running a hand through my hair, I shook out an alarming amount of dirt and some kind of bug encased in cobweb. I could smell the sweat on my clothes, and on a day like this, that odor could only get worse.

As I sat there curled into a ball, I let myself consider the worst-case scenario: the possibility that Ted would come back and kill me. He might not want Bill to know, but my death would certainly simplify things for him. I thought Ted was a guy who liked things simple.

Biting my lip, I tried to hold onto my courage. I did not want to die—and certainly not in my present condition. Dying at fifty is hard enough. Dying unkempt, stinky, and filthy is just wrong.

Chapter Twenty-one

Faye

I had serious reservations about spending the afternoon helping Dina Engel. I'd rather have gone with Barb, but if I was being watched, we couldn't afford to tip our hand. I certainly wasn't interested in attending the afternoon sessions, *Still Sexy* and *Knees Up!*, apparently some new kind of exercise instruction. Continuing my observation of Dina was the most productive use of my time.

Since the show was a highlight of the retreat, it would be held in the biggest space available, the dining room. A woman with a badge that said Love-Able Ladies Staff was guarding the door to keep the curious out, but when I said Dina had invited me, she let me go inside. I stood near the door for a few seconds, unsure what to do. The inn staff was finishing clean-up from lunch, but I noticed them glancing with raised brows at a group of newcomers who sat at a table near the back. Ten young women listened with varying degrees of interest while a man with his back to me talked earnestly to them. Dina wasn't there, but I saw immediately that at least some of her fears were justified. Pink, green, and lavender hair colors stood out—not exactly what this retreat's clientele would relate to.

The man, who hadn't yet noticed my entry, was about thirty years old. He wore a t-shirt that said *30 Seconds to Mars*, skinny jeans, and turquoise flip-flops. Moving confidently and speaking in a slightly affected way, he pantomimed with wide gestures, helping the models visualize where things would be tomorrow. I moved closer in order to hear what he said.

"Your dressing area will be here." He indicated the corner where they sat. "When you come out you'll walk through here—" He came toward me, along a narrow pathway through the dining tables, "—take a sharp left, and climb the steps on this end—" He ascended the left side of the dais in full model mode, face blank and shoulders thrown back to an almost impossible angle, "—and cross to center."

The women giggled at his posing, and he stopped in the center and swept his arms forward, palms up. "There'll be a short runway here. I want you to go out to the very, very end, do your best turn—no crotch shots, Gail—and exit on the other side. Follow the right-hand wall back to the dressing area and change into your next outfit. Got it?"

Nine pairs of eyes had followed his journey. Eight heads nodded. One woman seemed to be napping, and one was apparently the type who never ignores the invitation to ask a question. "What if we don't have enough time to change before it's our turn again, Honny?"

Honny—Roger Engel's appointed guardian of Dina's interests, rolled his eyes. "It's your job to get changed in time." Perhaps to soften the comment he added, "You have to do like Eliza Doolittle would say and 'Move your bloomin' arse.'"

The girl frowned, looking around at her companions. "Who's Eliza? I don't think I've met her."

The other girls tittered, but the questioner didn't give up. "Are they going to put a mirror back there so we can see how we look before we come out?"

Honny set his hands on his hips, a little too far back and stagey. "Sweetie, I'll be there, and I'm better than any mirror. I'll tell you when you've got the right look."

Pouty lips indicated she wasn't satisfied with that, but Honny went on. "Other concerns?"

When no one else spoke he said, "As soon as Dina gets here we'll do a walk-through so we can time it. Remember, the runway will be there in the morning, so take that into account."

He left them then, and as unobtrusively as possible, I moved to a spot where I could see the women's faces as they talked. I made myself look busy with a notepad and pen from my purse and without appearing to, listened intently to what they had to say.

There were three groups of two, one of three, and the girl who'd asked the questions, who sat off by herself. She had the pink hair, and tattooed leaves climbed out the front of her shirt and twined down her arms, like a storybook character who's slowly turning into a tree.

Beside her but a little apart sat two women who brought to mind a cousin of Dale's who owns her own Harley, cuts wood for a living, and smokes fat Cuban cigars at family gatherings while she criticizes anyone "dumb enough" to live in Allport. These women's tats were all barbed wire and bullets, and their skimpy tank tops concealed very little. Their expressions signaled a tendency to look for someone or something to dislike.

Behind them was the group of three Asian women with heavy-on-the-eye-liner eyes. They were slightly built, and I guessed they had thigh gaps large enough to drive a Humvee through. They'd certainly present a fitting problem for Dina. The one nearest me had the lavender hair I'd noticed earlier. Another had glitter down one whole side of her face in a Harlequin pattern. It made my skin itch to look at it.

The next couple was surprisingly normal-looking. Neither had obvious body revisions; neither wore the amount of make-up the others did. They were of average size, which meant they wouldn't be too hard to dress for the show. One seemed slightly lost, and the other spoke to her in low tones.

One girl had managed a hair color I'd call Irish Hills, since her head called to mind the putting surface at a championship golf course. She had a collection of metal art threaded through her face that horrified me, though I realized that was exactly the purpose. Her companion appeared normal until you noted two things—both of them on her chest. No one grows something like that on her own, and despite having seen *A Chorus Line* (twice, thanks to Retta) I didn't understand why any woman would buy herself "a fancy pair" that size.

"Who's that?" It was the curious, pink-haired woman, and she was pointing at me.

They all turned to stare, some hostile, some hardly interested. "Dina asked me to help with fittings," I said with as much confidence as I could muster.

"Oh. Wardrobe manager." She seemed proud to know the term, so I didn't contradict her. What would I say anyway? *Not a wardrobe manager, just an amateur in way over her head*?

One of the women I'd thought of as "Normal" spoke. "Honny went to get hotel staff to help unload the truck. I think Dina's out there too."

"I'm sure there's a lot to bring along for something like this."

"Yeah." It was one of the two I'd dubbed "Biker Babes" in my head. "We brought all kinds of sh—"

A glance from the first woman made her pause, but Biker Babe's glare said she didn't like being shushed. Ms. Normal's left eyebrow rose slightly, signaling she didn't really care. The Babe went on, "We didn't bring nobody to help with setup, so he's out there offering the valets twenty bucks to schlepp the stuff in here for him. Dumbass shouldna been such a cheapskate!" She glanced defiantly at Normal, who turned her gaze away pointedly to stress that she was ignoring her.

I guessed they'd been warned, probably by Honny, to keep their conversation civil. Biker Babe #1 looked at Babe #2 and rolled her eyes. One of the Asian women said something to her companions in her native language. The tone was critical, but I had no idea if she was disparaging me, Ms. Normal, or the Babes. One of them giggled in response. The third frowned as if to remind them not to be rude.

"I'm Cecily," Ms. Normal said. She poked the woman beside her, who opened her eyes. "This is Candice, but she's not feeling very well."

Now that I saw her up close, I realized that "Not feeling well" meant Candice was so stoned she couldn't focus. Though she made a half-hearted attempt at a smile, I wasn't sure she even knew I was there.

The woman with green hair and metalwork spoke up. "She'll be okay tomorrow. She gets carsick, so she took some medicine before the trip." She looked me directly in the eye as she told the lie. "I'm Bibi."

The Asian woman made another remark, and again her friend tittered. The third one chose to ignore her this time, as if by doing so she could minimize the impact of her behavior. "I'm Gwen." Her smile was genuine, and it shone through the thick makeup to reveal what I thought was a hint of shyness. "Not really, but no one here can pronounce my real name. This is Li, and that's Jun." Jun was the sly commenter, and Li the lavender-haired beauty.

"I'm Pixi—no *e* on the end," the pink-haired woman said. "The mouthy one is Gail and that's her twin, Dail. And the one with the hooters is Penny, but she dances as Plenny, for reasons you can prolly guess." Gail and Dail applauded, and Plenny gave them a mocking bow.

As I considered taking up my bag and running, Dina came through the kitchen doorway. Behind her were the inn's two valets, lugging in carts loaded with trunks, dress racks, and boxes whose contents I could only guess at. They set to work unloading in the back corner while Dina came forward to greet me.

"You're here." Turning her back to the women she added softly, "As you can see, I'm going to need all the help I can get." To the group she said, "This is Faye, who's going to figure out how to make the clothes fit you. Once we've got all the boxes unpacked we'll start, so you might want to take this time to visit the ladies' room." She pointed. "It's out that door." From a large bag slung over her shoulder she took a box of wipes and a box of zipper storage bags and held them out. "Start by taking off every bit of makeup and removing whatever piercings you've got that are removable. We'll go from there."

There were moans of protest, but Dina raised a hand. "When this is over, if we pull it off, I'll add a bonus to what you were promised." That pleased them, and the murmurs of discontent ebbed. "Now, has anyone here had experience with modeling?"

"I played a model in a film once," Pixi responded.

"Porn don't count," Dail informed her, and the others tittered appreciatively.

Dina shot me a glance, but Cecily spoke up. "I did some runway work a few years back."

Gail muttered something, and Dail grinned. Dina ignored them. "Could you hang around for a minute so we can talk?"

Gail said something I couldn't make out, but it was certainly nasty. Cecily's lips tightened, but she nodded assent.

"The rest of you get ready," Dina ordered. "Remember—no makeup, no metal—and don't leave the rest room in a mess." She pointed toward the doors, and some of the women rose. Beside Cecily, Candace remained seated, her eyes half closed and her muscles slack.

"What am I supposed to do with her?"

Dina's question was rhetorical, but Cecily answered, "She'll be okay tomorrow. I promise."

"She ain't lying," Bibi said. "Cecily can get Candace straight when it's important."

"I guess she can stay where she is for now." As she turned away, Dina locked eyes with me as if to say, "What can I do?"

Dail and Gail tossed disgusted glances backward as they left the room, Gail raising her little finger and making a face that simulated "La-di-dah" airs. Dina waited until they were gone then moved to where Cecily sat. "Tell us about your experience as a model."

Her eyes flickered once around the large room, and I got the sense Cecily tried not to think about her past. "I worked for Tybalt Talent, starting when I was sixteen. I did several trips to Europe and a lot of shows in the States: Detroit, of course, Chicago, New Orleans, and New York once." Her voice was almost wistful as she listed the places she'd appeared. How did a woman go from modeling high fashion to dancing nude in one of Roger Engel's seedy clubs?

Sensing the question Cecily said, "I developed a nose problem."

"Drugs." Dina's matter-of-fact tone said she'd seen others with promising futures go down that path of self-destruction.

"There was a guy. It's just that simple." She shrugged away any excuses, but her expression said it wasn't simple at all. "I got past it, but once you've disappointed people a few times, they don't let you back into their world." She glanced at Candice. "Unless someone comes along to help, you spiral down until your brilliant career is just a reflection in the rear view mirror."

"Who helped you?"

She smiled. "Honestly? I did. I looked at myself one day and all of a sudden it was like the old me asked the druggie me, "Why are you doing this to yourself?" She shifted in the chair. "I still work at it."

"The will to change has to come from inside." I thought Dina spoke as much for herself as for Cecily, and their eyes met briefly in shared understanding. After a second Dina asked, "Can you help me get these women ready for tomorrow?"

Cecily grinned. "I wasn't sure how you planned to do a fashion show with this bunch."

"Apparently this is my father's way of saving money." Dina grimaced. "I'm going to do this no matter what he pulls."

Pressing her lips together, Cecily considered. "There's a lot to get done."

"I know." Dina waved a hand at the boxes around us. "Honny will have to handle setting up the room. Roger didn't see the need to send real help for that either." She paused to bring her anger back under control. "Faye will take notes about what needs altering, and I'll make the changes tonight. Your part would be teaching the women how to conduct themselves like models. Can you do that?"

"I can if you put the fear into them." Cecily glanced at her drug-dazed friend. "I'm not very popular at the club since I turned into what they consider a Goody Two Shoes."

"I'll make things clear right now," Dina promised. "We'll have a little conference in the bathroom while they scrub their faces."

When she left us, Cecily turned to me. "How did you get dragged into this?"

"Lost my mind for a minute," I replied with a grin. "I mentioned I could sew, and the next thing I knew I was here."

"Doing triage."

"Dina will have a lot to get done tonight."

She thought about that. "Gwen makes a lot of our costumes." Blushing, she added, "Not that there's much to them, but she'd probably help if Dina waved a little cash at her. She's studying to be a teacher, so she always needs money."

My surprise slipped out before I could stop it. "A teacher?"

She grinned. "You thought we were all sluts and morons, right?"

It was my turn to blush. "Sorry. Too many cop shows on TV."

"Some of us have a future." In a moment of honesty she added, "Or we did once upon a time."

"It's not too late for you," I said impulsively. "Now that you're off—now that you've taken charge of your life, you can start making new pathways for yourself."

She shook her head. "I'm not getting any younger, and modeling is a young woman's game." Glancing at the boxes around us, she banished thoughts of her own future. "Right now we need to figure out how to help Ms. Engel make this work."

The door opened and Dina came toward us. "I made it clear you're in charge," she told Cecily. "Faye, let's look at the outfits. I have the descriptions on note cards, so I can put them in any order we need to."

The Asian trio had reappeared and taken seats. Gail and Dail hovered near the doorway, shooting daggers at Cecily with their eyes. "I'll make my own trip to the ladies and be right back," Cecily promised. Pausing she added, "I'm not great with makeup, but I think Li could help with that if you have Gwen ask her. Li's English isn't very good, but her skills with a brush are."

"I'll do that. Thanks."

Dina and I moved to where Honny and a valet from the inn had set up a long clothing rack. Opening a trunk, she began putting outfits already on hangers onto the crossbar. "We have thirty outfits. Accessories are attached to the hangers. You will need to decide who wears each one."

I looked at her in horror. "Me? I'm not—"

Qualified? Interested? Able? All of the above? This was such a Retta thing. If she were here to take over, she'd be thrilled and I'd be relieved.

Dina seemed to read my mind. "I'll help when I get the chance. Just make the best decisions you can."

Sweat prickled at my bra line. My "best decisions" usually involved whether to put on my dark blue mom jeans or the stone-washed ones.

"They'll each have three changes," she was saying. "I'd like the last round to be the outfits on the green hangers. They're my best work, and I want to do an array with all ten models as a finale."

Most of the women had returned, and they crowded around to get a look at what they'd be wearing. "I want that pink dress," Pixi demanded. "It'll look great with my hair."

"In the first place," Dina replied, "Faye decides who wears what. In the second place, your hair isn't going to be pink tomorrow."

Rebellion flared in Pixi's expression, but apparently the compensation she'd been promised was worth a little discretion. I wondered how Dina could pay the extra if her father was keeping a tight rein on the budget, but that wasn't my concern.

Cecily returned from her pit stop and called the group to the front of the room, where she began demonstrating how they would stand, turn, and walk. "A fashion show is about the clothes," I heard her say. "The audience isn't here to see you, but to imagine themselves looking as good as you do in the outfit you're modeling."

Beside me Dina said softly, "When I told them Cecily would show them how to walk, Pixi said, 'I've been walking since I was a year old. What can that old bag teach me?'" She chuckled. "Cecily's an 'old bag' at twenty-five? What does that make me?"

"Or me? I'm twice her age." I looked to where Cecily was executing a smooth, graceful turn as the models watched, their expressions doubtful. Dail and Gail looked downright grumpy, probably because they knew they could never achieve a similar result.

Leaving Cecily to her work, Dina began sorting outfits into piles, looking critically at the models as she made each decision. "You might have to switch things around," she said when she'd made tentative decisions. "If a whole outfit doesn't work, switch it to a different girl, even if they whine." I was feeling less confident by the second, but she went on. "If you can make the changes with safety pins, feel free. Anything I don't have to do tonight will help."

I felt compelled to issue a warning. "Dina, I've never worked with fabric like this. What if I ruin your beautiful things?"

She touched my arm reassuringly. "We either have to make them work or cancel the show." Her eyes, which I'd thought were soft blue, turned icy. "I will have some things to say to Roger when this is over."

"Did he explain to you why he did this?"

She made a dismissive noise. "He and I don't talk since he moved his latest girlfriend into our home and into—" Stopping herself from completing that thought, she finished instead with, "It's too late for him to fix this weekend, but I will have it out with him when I get home."

Honny had come up behind us, and his face revealed he'd heard. "Dina, your dad's just trying to make sure you stay in the black. He's a businessman, and he wants things run efficiently."

"He sabotaged my show, Honny. If people walk away tomorrow saying it was unprofessional—which it's likely to be—I'll have an uphill battle to overcome the negative comments these women will spread all over the state."

Honny hesitated, perhaps unsure where his loyalties were supposed to lie. Finally he executed a shrug worthy of a professional mime. "You know how he gets."

"I do." A crash sounded, and we looked over to where Candice had tripped going up the steps. Gail and Dail laughed uproariously, and the Asians tittered as she staggered to regain her balance. "Roger's fine with me dealing with a bunch of amateurs if it saves him a buck."

I was in that category, but seeing her so close to despair, I wanted to relieve Dina's mind. Honny apparently did too, because he patted her shoulder. "It's like they say, good help is hard to find, but I did what I could, given your dad's—um—decisions"

"Just make sure the room is set up correctly," she replied coldly. "I don't need to find out the mic doesn't work or the lighting is wrong."

I felt a little sorry for Honny, between the proverbial rock and a hard place as he tried to help Dina and still follow her father's orders. "I'll take care of it," he told her. "I promise to do my part."

And he did. As I worked through the afternoon, Honny was everywhere. His artistic persona and wide gestures made it easy to locate him whenever I looked up from my work. Even when I didn't seek him out I heard the slaps of his flip-flops as he moved around the room, operating with cool efficiency. First he spoke to the man in charge of the wait staff. Together they moved around the room, and from their gestures I guessed they were working out details of how the show and the luncheon would meld smoothly. When he left, Honny spoke to another man, and after a moment I recognized him: Bill. After explaining something while pointing at the ceiling, he led Honny to a bank of switches at the back of the room and demonstrated how he could change the illumination during the show.

Tucking my head into my chin, I kept working. Would Bill notice me? Would he care that I was helping Dina instead of attending the sessions like the other guests? And more importantly, since he was here, where was Retta?

If Bill saw me, he gave no indication. He and Honny experimented for a few minutes to get the effects Honny wanted. Once the lighting was planned, they stepped onto the dais, where Honny gestured in his loose-limbed, dramatic fashion. With a nod, Bill picked up the lectern and set it off to one side of the dais. Then he left for a while and returned with an extension for the microphone cord. When hooked to the existing one, it reached the lectern in its new spot, where Dina would stand, visible to the audience but not upstaging the fashions or getting in the models' way.

If Dina noted Honny's diligence, she was too unhappy to acknowledge them. He took it well, I thought. He even seemed to find her anger amusing, like when your little sister pouts because she isn't tall enough to ride the Sky Monster with her two older siblings.

Chapter Twenty-two

Barb

Retta was missing. Faye was closed in a room, hopefully safe with Dina Engel and her models. What should I do?

What I wanted to do was talk to Rory, not only my significant other but an experienced cop who'd become my sounding board when a case got complicated. But Rory was in Chicago, and I knew he and his daughter planned a shoreline cruise that afternoon.

Dale wasn't a good option either, though he was no doubt waiting to hear from me. Since he was physically unable to provide the help we needed, I sent him a text that would relieve his mind: *Talked to Faye. She's fine. Will call later with details.*

Since he was in New Mexico Lars had a distinct disadvantage, but he was FBI and he cared about Retta. He and Auburn had been friends, so he might know something about the case that would help. Finding his direct number in my contacts, I called.

Voicemail was my answer, so I left a message and went downstairs, hoping to see Faye so I could tell her what had happened.

The common area was quiet. The perfume girl I'd noticed earlier was focused on her phone. Sessions were ongoing, so everyone else was engaged. From one room came the sound of a blender, and I wandered over to read the sign: *Satisfying Meals for Two.*

"Excuse me." I turned to find a well-groomed—make that exquisitely groomed—woman at my elbow. In the tradition of Love-Able Ladies, she wore a skirt, not pants. Her blouse had a modest neckline, and her pumps were low-heeled and paired with nylon stockings. In a firm but not belligerent manner she said, "I don't see your badge."

"My—" I realized she meant the pin-on name-tag conference attendees were given. "I'm not part of the retreat."

"I see." Her expression said she'd already known that. "May I help with something then? This is a private event, and we booked the entire inn for the weekend."

There was no way I'd claim to be an admirer of Love-Able Ladies. "I just stopped to look the inn over, to see if I might want to stay here some time."

"I see. It's just that we got a report of a vandal defacing our signage." Her direct gaze made it clear to me that the perfume girl had been paying attention after all.

"That's too bad." I didn't specify if the tragedy was vandalism or the witnessing of same. What was she going to do—have me arrested for printing?

She raised a brow. "Apparently the writer fancies herself a feminist."

"By *feminist* you mean women who believe the radical notion that they're as good as men?"

"We all have strengths," she said primly, "but ladies don't try to *be* men."

"They accept secondary status and less pay for the same work?"

She pursed her lips before answering, as if willing herself to be patient. "It isn't a question of being primary or secondary. Men and women have different jobs to do."

Even with my sister missing, I wasn't inclined to let this ruffled, permed "lady" lecture me. "Then you'd agree with Timothy Leary that women who seek to be equal with men lack ambition?"

She completely missed the sarcasm. "Ambition is the *problem*. Why should women attempt masculine roles when we're so perfectly suited to being mothers and wives?"

"I don't know," I said with an exaggerated shrug. "Self-fulfillment, maybe?"

She tried to appear patient, but her tense jaw belied that. "By holding some job that stresses her until she's no fun to be around?" She waved a hand, conjuring an image. "A woman who seeks fulfillment might create a home business that provides an outlet for her creativity while still allowing her to be there for her children when they need her."

"But if we only do *home* business, *side* business, *small* businesses, men consider us less intelligent and therefore less important." I kept my voice low, but it took effort. "Do you realize women could once be put in asylums for questioning their husbands' authority? Do you know in our parents' generation a man could divorce a woman if she didn't have sex with him as often as he wanted it?"

The woman—her badge said Angel—seemed at a loss for words, so I went on. "I'm not willing to go back to the days when men assumed that because we're physically smaller, we're weaker in all ways." I shouldn't have gone on, but I did. "And I have a hard time tolerating women who do."

Her chin lifted. "Then perhaps you shouldn't be here."

"I have every right—"

"You have the right," she interrupted, "but is it fair of you to inflict your views on us? You aren't a member of our group. You didn't pay the fee that everyone else did." She touched the badge on her blouse. "We don't follow you around and harass you, so why do you think it's permissible for you to harass us?"

She had a point. I was invading space they'd reserved for their event. In addition to that, our argument was counterproductive to my purpose. I took a deep breath. "All right. I'm going."

I walked away angry with myself for calling attention to my presence. Now they'd be on the lookout for the "vandal" in their midst, so I'd have to avoid the retreat organizers *and* search for Retta. How much help would I be if I got ejected from the St. Millicent premises?

As I stepped into the bright sunlight and blazing heat outside the inn, my phone rang. Lars. Thoughts of gender inequity dissipated like smoke, and I leaned my rear against a decorative wine cask set near the doors. "Hey, Barb," he said when I answered. "What's up?"

"I'm in Traverse City, and we've got trouble." I told him briefly what had happened. The death of Agent Auburn was a shock, and the news Retta was missing brought a moan of anguish.

"I warned Chet," he said when I finished. "He was a little off the reservation on this one."

"You mean he was operating illegally?"

"No. Chet isn't—he wasn't that type. But I don't think his superiors were fully in the loop." Lars paused, and I pictured him running a hand through his light, slightly thinning hair. "I guess everybody in the Detroit office wants to see Engel arrested. Chet wanted to be the one who nailed him."

"How much was he doing on his own?"

"I'm pretty sure his supervisor knew he hoped to get Dina Engel's help. I don't think Chet told him he'd recruited your agency to approach her."

"Which means he was the only one protecting my sisters."

"In his defense," Lars said, "it shouldn't have been a dangerous situation."

"But now he's dead."

"Yeah." I heard the brush of fabric as he shifted in his chair. "Have you called the cops?"

"I intend to, but I'd like to find Retta first and get her out of the line of fire. We don't know who these people are, what they're after, or even how many of them there are. Faye could be in danger too."

"I can get you some help, but they'll need time to get there." He paused. "Barb, you don't believe they'll let Faye and Retta go when whatever they're planning is over, do you?"

"No. They're witnesses in the murder of a government agent."

He seemed relieved to hear I had no illusions about honor among murderers. "If this fashion show is when things are going to happen, we have less than twenty-four hours." He paused. "It's probably safer for Faye if you get her out of there."

I shook my head, though he couldn't see it. "She won't leave if it means putting Retta in danger. She'll keep doing what they tell her to until we figure something out."

"I understand that, but—"

"She's safe at least until four this afternoon. After that we'll re-evaluate."

"You're going to look for Retta, aren't you?"

"I'm going to *find* Retta," I corrected.

"Okay. I'll get somebody up there ASAP."

"Thanks."

His voice got husky. "I wish I were there to help."

"Me, too, Lars," I said. "Me, too."

Chapter Twenty-three

Retta

After what seemed like a year, I heard a key turn in a lock. A chain slid with a metallic rattle, and a rectangle of sunlight blinded me. Shielding my eyes, I saw Bill, who had bent to pick up the cardboard take-out container and bottle of water he'd set on the ground.

"I brought you lunch," he said as he entered the shed, "but it's kind of weird-looking. I just took what I could sneak out of the kitchen."

Opening the container, I found a fish taco half-buried by a scoop of coleslaw. "That's ahi tuna," he said proudly, "with jicama slaw—whatever that is."

"HEE-cama," I corrected. "The *j* is pronounced like an *h*."

"Oh. Well, that's what your sister had for lunch."

I guessed Faye hadn't been particularly pleased. She's a red meat-and-potatoes type of girl.

"What kind of wine?"

"Huh?"

"What wine did they serve with the ahi?"

"Um, the leftover stuff in the glasses was kinda pink."

"Rosé." I looked at him hopefully, but he hadn't brought any along. I took a big drink of water and then tried the slaw, which was lovely. "What time is it?"

Bill checked his watch. "Almost two."

I'd have sworn it was half-past six. "What have you been doing?"

"Helping the mic and lights guy set up for the fashion show tomorrow. Nice guy, but a little—you know." He dangled a hand, but when I didn't smile, he coughed and stuck it in his pocket.

"It was nice of you to bring me this," I said, "even if the taco's a little soggy." He looked deflated, so I took a bite to show my appreciation.

He noticed the state of my clothes and hands. "You're all dirty."

"This isn't exactly the Holiday Inn." After another bite I asked, "Do you think you could bring me some stuff from my hotel room?"

"Stuff?"

"My hairbrush and a wet cloth for my face and hands."

"How am I supposed to get that without somebody noticing?"

I'd thought about that. "Faye brought along a plain black tote bag for her books, and it's got straps, like a backpack. Empty that and put my stuff in it." When he looked doubtful, I held out my hands. "I can't stand being so dirty. You're the only one who can help me."

He opened his mouth a few times then gave up. "I can try, I guess."

I flashed him a big smile. "You're the best."

When he was gone I tested the doors, but he'd fastened the chain as tightly as before.

Maybe next time he'd be less careful.

Chapter Twenty-four

Faye

I stood in the right back corner of the room—which tomorrow would be enclosed with movable panels—ready to assess what needed to be done. After some preliminary demonstrations of turns and poses, Cecily went through the whole course, starting from the back of the room and moving to the front, striding confidently across the dais, and stepping gracefully down the other side without once glancing at her feet. The others watched critically, but Dina expressed satisfaction. "That's exactly how it should look. Let's see the rest of you do it."

While they lined up, Cecily hurried back to where I waited. "Dina said I should put on my first outfit. Once they practice the walk and the poses, we'll try it again, wearing the clothes."

I selected a hanger. "Here's one Dina thought would fit you."

Cecily began undressing with no apparent concern, though Honny knelt only a few feet away, putting tape down to mark where the panels would go. I turned away, watching as Plenny entered from the left, went up the steps to the platform, and started across. "Stop there," Dina ordered. "Turn. Slower, please. Okay, that's not too bad."

I'd been thinking it was really bad. Plenny moved like a tween in her first bra, all strut and no subtlety. Still, it was a start.

"Next!" Dina's voice got stronger as she immersed herself in the project. "No," she ordered Li. "Don't smile. Look over the heads of the audience as if they aren't there." Li giggled nervously, putting a hand over her mouth and squinting her eyes.

Bibi came next, doing a pretty good job with her model stare but the walk—not so much. "Don't swing your hips," Dina ordered. "Keep everything straight and in line."

"You mean like I got a stick up my—"

"Straight!" Dina interrupted. "You aren't working to get a twenty stuffed in your G-string."

Dail leaned toward her sister and said something that made Gail guffaw, but the steel in Dina's voice pleased me. She was more confident than I'd first thought, at least when it mattered to her. In an industry as competitive as fashion, that was good.

Cecily stepped into the dress I'd handed her as she watched the action. "It's kind of fun to be back," she said wistfully. "Wish I hadn't screwed up so bad."

"If I've learned anything from living," I told her, "it's that looking backward doesn't get you where you want to be."

"Yes, but—"

"You made some mistakes," I interrupted. "Focus on what you'll do now, not what you did then."

"You're right." She turned her back so I could zip her into the semi-fitted, cream-colored dress. Not only had Dina made a good guess as to the fit, it was perfect with her dark hair and coffee-colored skin. Taking the bag of accessories from the hanger, I helped with the necklace while she threaded incredibly long earrings through her lobes.

"Where did the jewelry come from?"

"Great, isn't it? I heard Dina say she has an old friend from college who designs costume jewelry. She plans to use her stuff all the time."

"What about shoes?" I asked. "Where are the shoes that go with the outfits?" Frowning, I added, "I never thought how much goes into putting on a show like this."

Cecily chuckled. "You mean when it's done right, or the way we're doing it?" She pointed to a large plastic tub. "What we've got for shoes is in there."

I opened the tub to find a jumble of footwear, each pair connected with plastic thread. They were new, but they definitely didn't look like accessories for *haute couture* to me.

"Here are the rest." Honny's voice came from behind me, and I turned to find him opening a second tub of shoes. He seemed embarrassed but explained, "Mr. Engel cancelled Dina's shoe order and suggested we stop and buy shoes at Shoes-a-Rama on the way north. He said nobody will be looking at their feet."

I was disliking Roger Engel more and more. "Cheap shoes, amateur models, no one to help load and unload. Is that how he contributes to his daughter's success?"

Honny touched the shaved area above his ear. "You'd have to know Mr. Engel to get it."

Sorting through the tub, Cecily tossed rejected shoes onto the lid to get them out of her way. "We each got to pick two pairs of dress shoes and one pair of boots." She held up a cheap shoe, adding, "Woohoo!"

"I figure the girls can mix and match for tomorrow and keep the shoes afterwards." Though Honny seemed proud of his bargains, even a novice like me knew this was no way to run a fashion show.

When she was dressed, Cecily hurried to the front. As I expected, there was a spirited discussion of the shoes she wore. It was probably a good thing Honny had left the room, or he would have got an earful. Dina shot me a despairing look, but I gave her a thumbs up. Cecily looked good, and I changed the thumb to a "one," indicating my opinion she should be the first model. Dina nodded agreement.

Cecily demonstrated the walk again, highlighting the costume's attributes as they were described. I didn't get to see all of it, since Dina had shooed Dail in my direction. I turned to the rack, hoping the outfit we'd chosen would soften some of her hard edges. Her ink showed through the thin fabric of her blouse, but Dina had said the problem would be addressed. So many problems. So little time.

Halfway through the first round of fittings I had developed a fairly smooth system. I handed each woman an outfit generally suited to her size and coloring. Once she put it on, I made an assessment. If there was a major problem with the fit, I made notes for Dina. If only a tuck or two was required, I made the alterations myself, using safety pins or a few stitches. At one point I borrowed Honny's duct tape to close slits I'd made in the side seams of a top. The stuff was as useful for quick clothing repairs as it is everywhere else in life.

Only once did Dina disagree with my choice, and the model involved was Plenny. Since there was almost a twenty-inch difference between her bust size and her waist, I had to switch tops with another outfit. It worked, but Dina's sharp eye caught the substitution.

Leaving Cecily in charge, she hurried back to me. "I'm not fond of the black shirt with the brown pants."

When I explained the problem, she nodded. "Let me see what I brought for extras." Sifting through the rack, she located a long, swingy black jacket. "Put her in the emerald blouse that goes with the pants, then cut it up the back. Do whatever it takes to make it look okay, then put this over it to hide the damage."

I did as she suggested, though it made me cringe to slice into the beautiful, expensive fabric. Plenny put the blouse on, and I stripped duct tape across the back to shape it to her unbalanced figure. The jacket covered the tape and added a touch of finish to the outfit—not that I thought myself a competent judge of such things. From her place at the front, Dina signaled that the look was good. When Plenny returned and took the blouse off, I lined the tape on the outside with more strips on the inside so it wouldn't stick to her skin during the show.

As the afternoon wore on, I did pretty well adjusting Dina's creations to the irregular forms of the models. They were a likeable bunch except for Dail and Gail, but nobody seemed to pay their sarcastic comments much mind. The Asian girls were tittery, at least two of them were. I guessed that was more from nerves than anything else. They'd been tossed into something they didn't understand, and their poor command of English made it even more difficult. They did okay, watching the others and doing as they did.

As I pinned and sewed, I worried about what was going on outside the world of Dina's preparations. Barb and Retta were probably talking to the police right now. They'd arrest Bill and Ted, ending whatever they had planned for tomorrow. When the rehearsal was over, I might be free to leave St. Millicent's and go home.

Once the women were dressed in their first outfits, Dina called for a timing. She served as moderator, reading her prepared comments from index cards. She had to make a few changes to account for the alterations, but all in all, Round One went well. Honny kept track with a stopwatch, and the models listened to Dina in order to match their movements to the descriptions. I caught only quick glances, since I'd already started fitting Cecily for her second outfit.

The Paisley tunic top was too big for her slim figure, so I pinned it along the seamlines. "Don't make any sudden moves until Dina has a chance to sew those in," I told her as she put on the matching cranberry leggings. "You'll suffer the death of a thousand pokes."

"It's often like that," she replied. "There were times when the outfits we wore were just basted together. You say a little prayer your skirt doesn't fall off halfway down the runway."

Round Two went okay, but again there were problems I couldn't camouflage or fix with pins and tape. "She'll be up all night," I told Cecily as we watched the others make their second pass around the room. They were getting the idea, though the twins' heavy footsteps echoed on the flimsy dais and Pixi's pink hair was jarring atop the sophisticated evening gown she wore.

"What is Dina going to do about the hair?" I asked.

"Honny will buy rinses when we get back to Traverse City. We'll end up with a lot of brunettes, but Dina thinks the audience will react better to that than to the rainbow we've got now."

"And the tattoos?"

"Stage makeup. There's good stuff out there now, because lots of people need to hide body art, like actors, job-seekers, and workers whose bosses frown on them."

Dina approached, her note cards in one hand and a pen in the other. "Cecily, when we're done here, would you take my car and make a trip to Traverse City for me?"

"And why am I going there?"

"I need a sewing machine, but Honny has no clue what to buy."

"And I do because I'm female?" Cecily arched a brow then chuckled to show she wasn't offended. "My grandma used to sew. I think I can handle it."

"Great. You can stay in my room tonight. I'll be sewing my little heart out anyway."

Cecily looked regretful. "I'd help with the alterations, but I can't do much beyond threading a needle."

Dina raised a hand. "Just get me that sewing machine then get a good night's sleep. You'll have plenty to do come morning."

The third round went well, with only a few pieces that needed significant resizing. When the parading was done, Dina had the models line up across the dais as a finale. Cecily's instruction had resulted in a more professional, less—I guess *commercial* was the word—group. Though the tension in Dina's shoulders remained, Honny's stopwatch revealed the show took just under thirty-nine minutes, almost exactly the time allotted.

Chapter Twenty-five

Barb

Lars had promised to email information on Roger Engel, so I got my tablet from the car and went upstairs to my sister's room. Using the inn's wi-fi, I found he'd come through for us.

> *Barb,*
>
> *I talked to the people in Detroit. Agent Tonya Holden wants you to meet her at six p.m. at an ice cream shop called Cherry Delite about a mile south of your location.*

I checked my watch. It was almost two. I had time to do some searching on my own before I met the agent.

> *Don't take these guys on yourself. Wait for Holden's arrival and do exactly as she says.*
>
> *Lars*

Attached to the email were documents he probably shouldn't have shared with me, reports of the Bureau's attempts to tie Roger Engel to drug importation. In several cases the disappearance or death of someone who could have testified against him stopped forward movement, and the case was left hanging. As a result, the Bureau had a mountain of suspicion but no proof they could use in court.

Could Dina Engel be using her fashion business to help her father move drugs into northern Michigan? There was a rumor reported that they were barely civil to each other. If she wasn't actively assisting Engel, might she be an innocent dupe? He seemed the type who might use his daughter's dream of success in fashion to further his own ends.

How did Auburn's death fit in? Had he become too eager and approached Dina himself? If so, he might have been murdered because of it. Whatever the reason for his death, the odds my sisters would live through the weekend weren't good, since they'd happened along at precisely the wrong moment.

Faye was trying to figure out Dina Engel's motives in coming to St. Millicent's. I hoped she could do that soon, before Retta suffered the same fate as Chet Auburn.

There was one more concern in my mind. The FBI badly wanted to arrest Roger Engel. I wanted my sisters to be safe. I wasn't sure that the two goals melded well. While the safety of private citizens is taken seriously by law enforcement, I'd seen lust for a big arrest mar the judgment of officers before. It would be best if I could locate Retta before six o'clock. Then the question of priorities would be resolved. Once she was safe, Agent Holden could do whatever was necessary to deal with Engel, his daughter, and his men.

They had to be holding Retta somewhere they could lock her in. An outbuilding seemed likely, one far enough away from the inn that she wouldn't be heard if she called for help. While I waited for the FBI to arrive, I could search the grounds for a likely spot. Since I was *persona non grata* to the Love-Able Ladies, it was best if I left their territory anyway.

Retta

I wasn't wearing my watch when we left the hotel room, so I had no idea what time it was when Bill showed up again. Hearing the chain rattle, I stood as he entered with Faye's black bag slung over his shoulder. "Here."

Opening the bag I found a hairbrush, a bottle of water, and a dampened hotel towel. "No clean clothes?"

He shuffled his feet. "It didn't feel right, going through your stuff."

Actually, that was kind of sweet. I drank some water then started with the towel, wiping my face and hands. "That feels better." Reaching into the bag again, I took out the brush. "Oh, dear."

"What?"

"That's Faye's hairbrush."

"So?" He seemed genuinely curious.

"Faye has thick, curly hair," I explained. "Mine is finer, with body but no curl."

"Oh." Clearly, the explanation hadn't helped.

"Faye's brush is too harsh for me." His frown deepened. "It's okay. I'll use it just this once." I went to work, brushing away grit and cobwebs.

Bill watched, looking pleased with himself. "There's a home-made cookie in the outside pocket."

I knew for a fact there had been a half-dozen. He'd helped himself to Faye's snickerdoodles and left me one. "That's nice for a snack," I said. "When are you bringing dinner?"

"Dinner? Lady—"

"My metabolism runs high," I told him, tilting my head a little to one side. "If I don't eat regular meals, I get light-headed."

"Tr-Ted says I can't be heading down here too often. Somebody's going to wonder why."

"Come after dark, so no one sees you. Ted doesn't need to know."

Bill wasn't the sharpest knife in the drawer, and he'd run out of excuses. He wasn't mean enough to look me in the eye and say I'd get no supper. His head drooped. "I'll see what I can do."

"Anything but lamb or veal," I told him. "I can't stand the thought of a baby on my plate."

Chapter Twenty-seven

Barb

Leaving the inn by the back entrance, I turned to the south, skirting the vineyard and taking to the trees along its edge. I guessed St. Millicent's had several outbuildings, but in the way of touristy places, they'd be tucked out of sight when possible. My theory was borne out as I passed two pole buildings, wooden frames covered with sheet metal, set into the trees along the edge of the rows. The doors of both were open, and it was evident there were no prisoners concealed inside. In the second one, a man stood with his back to me, putting tools into a knapsack. He looked the right age to be Bill, but I couldn't tell if he had the silver streak Faye had mentioned.

Tracing the rows of grapevines, I climbed to the top of the rise, which was farther from the inn than it appeared. The day had grown hot, and I soon wished I'd brought along a bottle of cold water and the baseball cap I keep in my car. The trellised vines, lined row on row with strips of grass in between, made it difficult to see across the sprawling property, and the forest on my right might have hidden a dozen buildings from view. I should have asked the man in the pole barn where the outbuildings were on the property.

I turned to look behind me. It was a long trek back to the pole barns, and I weighed the value of better information against covering the distance a second time. As I vacillated, I heard voices. The plants screened the speakers from view, but after only a few words, I guessed I was listening to Ted and Bill.

"—coming and going," one man was saying. "She needed a hairbrush, but I brought the wrong one. And you should hear what she wants for dinner—"

He had to be talking about Retta.

"Why in hell do you care what she wants?" I guessed that was Ted.

As they passed between the rows, I caught glimpses of them. One was the man I'd seen in the pole building, and now that he faced me, I saw the silver streak. A strap slung over his shoulder secured a gas-powered pruner to his back like an arrow quiver, and atop it was the knapsack he'd been filling. In the pockets of his cargo pants were two water bottles, and he carried a stepladder on the opposite shoulder. He looked like the peddlers of old, carrying with them everything they might need.

Bill gestured widely with his free hand as he tried to explain my sister to his companion. "She makes you think you gotta do what she asks you to. You feel mean if you don't."

Now I *knew* Retta was the topic of conversation.

"*You* feel like that, because you're an idiot." Ted's voice got louder, and I ducked into the trees for fear he'd look my way. "I told you—no more trips back there to wait on that old bag."

"We could let her go," Bill said. "She said she wouldn't tell, and then I wouldn't feel like I had to—"

"Shut up!" Ted gestured angrily toward the opposite side of the vineyard. "I should just take care of her right now, so you can stop being a wuss and do what you're supposed to."

"No!" Bill seemed panicked to realize he'd put Retta in danger. "I'll ignore her from now on, honest."

I sensed Ted's disbelief. Apparently Bill did too, because he added, "She'll be okay out there until tomorrow, and then we'll let them go like you said, right?"

The pause that followed the question went on a hair too long. "Yeah," Ted finally said. "We let them go."

Chapter Twenty-eight

Retta

The chain on my prison door rattled, and I looked up to see Bill, who'd apparently been pruning. Twigs and leaves stuck to his shirt like decorations, and his face was damp with sweat. "Hot out there," he said. "How you doing?"

"Okay, I guess."

He took a bottle from his pants-leg pocket. "I brought you some more water."

I stood, dusting the rear of khaki pants that would never be the same again. "That's really nice of you."

Setting the water on the hood of the tractor, he backed away. "I came to tell you I can't come around anymore."

"Because of Ted?"

"Yeah. I got to look like I'm doing my inn job, and I got to be close in case he needs me for something."

"Like hauling away a dead body?"

His eyes rattled around in his head like dice. "I told you about that. The guy recognized Ted and came after him."

"Bill, do you really believe he's going to let me go? For that matter, do you think they're going to let you live after what you witnessed?"

"I can't tell on 'em, 'cause now I'm as guilty as Ted, according to the law." After a second or two of mental struggle, he repeated what he'd been told like a mantra. "They got no reason to hurt you. We'll be gone by noon tomorrow, so you can tell what you want to who you want. It won't matter."

I imagined Ted saying those very words to allay his fears. Bill had to know Ted was a liar, but believing him was easier than opposing him. We all choose the wrong path sometimes, and we often stick to our choice long after it stops making sense.

I had to think fast. "Could you do one thing before you go?"

"What's that?"

"That back corner is shady, so it's the coolest spot in this place, but there's a huge spider living there. I can't make myself go near it."

He peered in the direction I pointed. "A spider, huh? You know they don't hurt nothing."

"I can't help it—I'm terrified of them." I allowed a little tremor in my voice. My reward was the look a man gets when he can help some little ol' gal in a way that makes him feel manly but doesn't require much effort.

Squaring his shoulders like Jason facing Medusa, Bill started for the back of the shed. "Where's this scary critter?"

I led him to the spot and pointed out a web studded with long-dead insects. "It was in there. Watch out, because it's huge!"

"The bigger they are, the easier they squash." He bent down to peer at the mess.

"I can't watch." I backed away. "I hate it when they squish."

Intent on finding his quarry, Bill hardly noticed. I took a few more steps backward then broke into a run for the exit. I heard his surprised grunt of realization behind me, but I was almost there. Should I close the doors and try to lock him inside, or should I run into the woods and find a hiding place?

That question was never answered, because Ted stood just outside the shed. His presence barely registered before he clubbed me with a fist that sent me staggering backward. Luckily Bill had come up behind me, and he caught me before I fell onto the concrete floor.

"Saw you coming this way and figured you wasn't doing what I said," Ted said. "How many kinds of an idiot are you, anyway?"

"I brought her some water, and then she said there was a spider—" Bill stopped, aware now how thin my story had been.

"I ought to snap your neck right now." Ted leaned toward me with menace in his eyes.

"You said we'd let them go," Bill protested. "Remember?"

"Yeah," Ted replied, but his eyes revealed the lie. "Now do like I told you. Keep an eye on that woman I showed you with the black and purple hair. We need to make sure she doesn't leave the inn tonight." He pointed at me. "This one gets to live if you stop bringing her stuff and doing errands because she asks so nice. Got it?"

"Sure." Bill looked relieved. His eyes avoided mine, but he didn't meet Ted's gaze either. Things were going from bad to worse, but he didn't know what to do about it. Bill's quick exit told me I wouldn't see him again today. I was going to have to get out of this shed by myself.

Chapter Twenty-nine

Faye

When the rehearsal was done, the paraphernalia for the show had to be stored until morning. Dina had been given a small meeting room on the main floor, and she intended to remain there all night, making the alterations, ironing the pieces, and then putting the costumes together so it was easy to locate them during the show.

Honny had a bit of a tantrum when she announced her intention. Putting a hand on his heart like a silent movie star he said, "You have to get *some* rest, Dina. Promise me you'll go to bed at least by two."

She dismissed his concern with a wave. "I can always lay my head on the table for a few minutes if I get tired."

Clicking his tongue at her stubbornness, Honny gave up. Promising to be back by eight, he herded eight of the models out through the kitchen. Two stayed behind, Cecily, who'd soon be on a quest for a sewing machine, and Gwen, who'd agreed to help Dina with the alterations.

I'd picked up details of their arrangements from conversations overheard as I worked. Gail and Dail had come north in the property van, a vehicle stuffed with clothing, accessories, and supplies for the show. Honny had brought the rest of the girls in a party limo borrowed from Roger Engel's fleet. In yet another cost-saving measure, he'd booked rooms for the girls at a small motel outside Traverse City, quite a distance away but cheaper than rooms on the peninsula. In the bathrooms at that motel, certain hair color adjustments would be made before he brought them back to St. Millicent's in the morning.

"Make sure they sleep," Dina warned as the girls gathered their belongings and prepared to depart. "No partying all night."

Honny gave her a casual grin, as if any fears she entertained on that score were groundless. Still, I saw Cecily take Bibi aside and speak earnestly to her. They both glanced at Candace as they spoke, and Bibi nodded. I guessed she'd promised to watch over her for the night and try to assure she didn't take any of her "medicine" before the show.

When they were gone, Dina and I loaded a canvas crate full of clothing she'd be adjusting onto a hotel luggage cart, and the valet who'd been helping us took it to her little workroom somewhere down a hallway. She thanked me repeatedly for my help, and when I said I was sorry I couldn't stay longer, she waved away my apology. "Gwen seems to know what she's doing." She took up her phone, which she'd silenced for the duration of the rehearsal. "I've got a ton of messages and voicemails to answer. Thanks again, and I'll see you tomorrow."

I was again tempted to warn Dina about Bill and Ted. If their plan was to kidnap her to extort money from her father, she should know she was in danger. Bending to retrieve my purse from where I'd stashed it behind a chair, I lingered, fiddling with the strap as I tried to make a decision.

Dina had begun listening to her phone, deleting a message, and listening again. The hotel wait-staff had invaded the space as soon as it was clear the rehearsal was finished, making her task difficult. Carts piled with rattling dishes rolled by, and sharp snaps sounded as waiters shook out clean tablecloths. Dina's forehead creased as she tried to hear what was being said on the phone.

Still I hesitated. Was my confidence in Dina's innocence strong enough to put my sister's life at risk? I liked the designer, but being likable isn't the same as being honest. I might be wrong to think Dina was the target of the plot. Whatever was supposed to happen was slated for Sunday morning. In the end I decided to wait a bit and see what Barb found out.

I stopped outside the dining room, scanning the area. Barb wasn't there. Thinking she might be waiting in the rest room where we'd spoken earlier, I headed that way. As I went in, Cecily was coming out, and we did one of those awkward pauses when neither knows who should go first. Smiling, I stepped back, and she exited with a comment. "Pit stop before I take off on my quest for a sewing machine."

Eager for any scrap of information to help me make my decision, I asked Cecily, "Had you met Dina before today?"

"No. We've all met Mr. Engel, of course, and we all know Honny real well."

"How is that?"

She shifted her shoulders slightly. "Honny is kind of Mr. Engel's stand-in. He watches the clubs and makes sure there's no skimming or anything like that."

I looked at her doubtfully. "Honny doesn't look much like an enforcer."

"I'm not saying he breaks legs or anything. He's just always there, watching. Mr. Engel trusts him, so everybody wants Honny to be happy, so he'll say nice things about them to the boss."

"Dina told me Honny's her financial watchdog."

"From what I hear, Mr. Engel and Dina don't communicate. Honny has to act as go-between, and he says it gets pretty weird sometimes." Cecily backed away, waving. "I have to go buy a sewing machine. See you tomorrow."

As I watched Cecily walk away, I thought she was a very likeable young woman. I hoped today's success might give her the confidence to return to the world she'd fallen out of.

When I came out of the rest room a few minutes later, refreshed and hands clean, I still hadn't found Barb. What did that mean? If she'd managed to free Retta, they'd have been waiting for me. If she hadn't, she might be somewhere briefing law enforcement on the situation and helping them plan a rescue. Barb had taken my key. I'd have to go up to the room, knock on the door, and say I'd misplaced it.

A few women milled around the common area, looking at the merchandise and chatting idly. Probably to avoid the noise, Dina had moved to a spot under the staircase. She stood with her face to the wall, her phone to one ear and her hand over the other. I started up the stairs, and as I reached the landing where they made a ninety-degree turn, an odd thing happened. Dina's voice, undiscernible when we were on the same level, floated upward with amazing clarity.

"I'm not happy having these women on my hands."

In minutes, maybe seconds, one or the other of the sessions would recess and a hundred attendees would stream into the common area. Dina's voice would be buried in the babble. I wanted desperately to learn who "these women" were. The models who weren't models, or Retta and me?

Hardly daring to breathe, I stood with one foot on the landing and the other on the step, leaning back a little so she wouldn't see me if she happened to look up. "Tomorrow is important to me," she was saying, "but you really screwed things up."

Doors opened, and the noise level rose as women emerged from their session. I heard the last sentence only because Dina raised her voice slightly. "I'm not letting either of them go when this is over, so just deal with it."

Interpretations volleyed in my brain like a badminton shuttlecock. Had Dina been referring to the fashion show or something else— something so important an FBI agent had been murdered to hide it? The last part, about the two she wasn't going to let go, made me glad I hadn't told Dina my secret. If "either of them" was Retta and me, Dina Engel was much more sinister than I'd imagined her to be.

Chapter Thirty

Barb

The exchange I'd overheard between Bill and Ted convinced me Retta was somewhere on the opposite side of the vineyard. As the sun beat down on my head, I waited impatiently for them to go somewhere else. Again I wished I'd brought water along—at that point even tepid water would have been fine.

I was at the northwestern corner of the St. Millicent property, where signs facing the opposite way suggested that uninvited visitors should remain on their own side of the fence. I rested my back against the trunk of a thick oak as I waited, allowing the two men plenty of time to do whatever they were doing out there and head back to the inn. My position on high ground allowed me to see over the vineyard, and I tried to spot a structure on the other side that might hold a prisoner. At first I saw no evidence of outbuildings at all, but an anomaly too square to be natural finally caught my eye. Squinting, I detected what was possibly the peak of a gray-shingled roof. Under it, screened from clear view by trees, was what might be a cement-block building. Block construction suggested it was older, possibly left over from whatever the property was before it became a vineyard. A concrete shed would be a good place to close someone in who didn't want to be there.

Rejuvenated by hope, I started across the vineyard. On either side of me grapes hung in clusters, ripening but not yet ripe. I kept my eye on the roof peak as best I could, staying low and hoping the vines, wooden training stakes, and cross wires hid me from view. Retta makes fun of my affinity for dark clothing, but at least I wasn't an orange or red or yellow figure moving through the greenery. As I went, I listened for the sound of conversation or clippers. All I heard was my own soft footsteps and the clucking of a squirrel irritated by my passage.

The building was almost hidden by foliage, and I might have walked past it unaware if I hadn't seen the roof from the hilltop. It was old but sturdy, its only window covered by boards. The entry was on the side away from the vineyard, two large doors chained closed with a padlock.

I listened before tapping softly on the door. "Retta?"

After a second I heard movement inside. "Barbara? Is that you?"

"I'm going to get you out of there." I pulled at the chain, tested the doors, and checked my pockets for something I might use to pick the lock. Not that I knew how to pick a lock, but I was willing to make an attempt.

"Is there something in there you can use to pry at the door?"

"Do you think I didn't consider that, Barbara Ann?" At least she was still her snotty self. "There's nothing in here but an old tractor like Dad used to have."

"Can you start it?"

"It won't start."

"Are you sure?"

"No, I'm *not* sure! It's been forty years since I drove a tractor."

I had to admit I might not remember how it was done either. There'd been a system to it, steps that had to be done in order. "Wait. Remember Dad's mnemonic? He—"

Before I could say more, someone behind me put an arm around my waist and another at my throat, cutting off my breath.

"Nosy old bat, ain't you?"

A flash of blond hair in my peripheral vision revealed my assailant was Ted. I was at every disadvantage: surprised, weaponless, and twenty-five years older than he. I would have to fight for my life.

Suppressing that first moment of panic, I recalled my self-defense training. Though I hadn't used it often, I practiced at the local gym and took refresher courses whenever they were offered. The instructors advised hitting an attacker's vulnerable spots: eyes, knees, and groin. My position made connecting with his groin almost impossible, but I reached back with my fingers, clawing at Ted's eyes. At the same time, I kicked hard at the inside of his knee. My fingers never reached their target, but I managed to land a decent blow to the knee. Staggering backward, Ted fell to the ground, pulling me along with him. I landed on his chest, which sent the breath whooshing out of his lungs. His grip weakened as he fought for air, and I rolled out of his arms and got to my feet.

Attack or run? That question was decided when Ted began fumbling at the waistband of his jeans, where the butt of the gun showed dark against his white belly. I turned to run but had taken only a step when his hand closed on my ankle. I stopped short, falling forward onto the dirt. Something—a rock or a tree root—cracked painfully against my head, and the earth's rotation seemed to shift for a moment. Somehow, I delivered a sharp kick to his face with my free foot. His nose caught the brunt of it, and I heard a roar of pain. All that mattered to me was that he released my foot. Scrambling upright, I took off into the woods. As I ran, I heard Retta pounding on the wooden door and screaming, "Don't hurt her, you creep! Don't you hurt my sister!"

Chapter Thirty-one

Retta

Do you have any idea how terrible it is to know that someone you love is in mortal danger and not be able to do a thing about it?

When the commotion began outside the shed, I immediately recognized Ted's voice. I heard Barbara make a choking noise. Then he said some words no gentleman says in front of a lady. When he hollered like a gored bull it was impossible to tell exactly what had happened, but from the continued swearing, I deduced Barbara Ann had got away.

"Yes!" I did a little fist pump, but my happiness was short-lived. Ted wouldn't just let her run back to the inn. He'd go after her, and he was faster and meaner than she was. Though she'd have rolled her eyes at the idea, I said a little prayer for an angel to help Barbara find a place to hide in the woods where that monster couldn't find her.

Recalling what she'd said, I turned to the tractor. Could I get it started? Barbara had given me a hint, though she hadn't got it all out.

Dad liked mnemonics: little memory devices that help us recall information. HOMES is for the Great Lakes (Huron, Ontario, Michigan, Erie, Superior) and ROYGBIV is the spectrum (red, orange, yellow, green, blue, indigo, violet). I learned to spell arithmetic by chanting "A rat in the house might eat the ice cream" and geography with "George Eastman's old grandmother rode a pig home yesterday."

Dad had devised a mnemonic to help us remember the steps in starting the tractor, and I recalled it had something to do with traveling. The problem was he'd had a hundred of them, and I wasn't sure which one started the tractor. Closing my eyes, I tried to picture myself going through the motions. Then I tried to imagine Dad's voice in my ear, telling me what to do.

Those things kept getting edged out by more recent memories of Barbara outside the shed, struggling against that nasty Ted. Had she been chased down and stabbed to death, as Agent Auburn had been? Was she cowering somewhere while Ted crept through the woods, stalking her? Was she crashing through the trees with him in pursuit?

As long as those fears wouldn't leave my mind, the search for Dad's mnemonic, buried somewhere in my mind, was crowded out by dread.

Chapter Thirty-two

Barb

Expecting a bullet in my back at any moment, I crashed downhill through the trees, pushing branches out of my way when I could, accepting their lashes across my face and body when I could not. Swearing and heavy breathing behind me indicated Ted had recovered from my kick and come in pursuit. I zig-zagged to spoil his aim but knew I couldn't outrun him for long. Worse, in my haste to get away, I'd chosen the wrong direction, away from the inn. My pursuer was between me and help.

The descent turned steeper, and I had to watch my footing so I didn't fall and roll into a tree or a shelf of rock. I wished I'd worn something other than sandals, but at least these had straps that held them on my feet. Falling to a knee, I rose and struggled on, hearing my labored breathing as my lungs made an unaccustomed effort. Unlike the brisk walks Rory and I enjoyed, this was a flight from death.

The woods opened suddenly, and I stumbled onto the road. I'd come all the way down the hill and was now at the level of the bay, which twinkled between the trunks of a stand of trees on the opposite side. I looked both ways, but there was no one visible in either direction. Run back uphill, toward the inn, or hide and try to trick him into thinking I'd been picked up by a passing car?

Gasping for air, I realized I had no chance to win a race uphill. I'd hide in the trees and use my phone to call for help. Since a car might come by at any time, the smartest thing Ted could do was give up chasing me and make his escape.

The moment it took to make that decision was my downfall. I had just reached the far side of the pavement when Ted broke from the woods and spotted me. Now there was no time to get my phone out, no time to hide. Skidding on the gravel at the side of the road in my haste, I hurtled toward the grove of trees along the bay. The little copse was mostly pines, which meant low branches that scratched my face and arms and dragged against my pant legs as I pushed forward. My solace was that anything that slowed me down slowed Ted too.

Then there were no more trees. I stumbled onto the shore of the bay, a wide expanse of sand studded with small rocks. Having learned that delay wasn't an option, I kept running, heading toward the inn, but on the flat beach, not uphill. Once I was in sight of the inn he'd have to give up the chase, for anyone up there could look down and see us.

My lungs burned, and my legs felt close to collapse. When the view to the road opened up, I glanced to the side, hoping to see a vehicle, but there was none. Ahead, the roof line of the inn extended above another stand of trees. I doubted I could make it to the open spot in front of the inn before Ted caught me. It felt like he was closing in, though I didn't dare turn to look.

That's when I saw the canoe. Bright blue, it lay on its side on the beach ahead, next to a pretty little gazebo meant for moonlight trysts and daytime beach activities. The craft offered a chance running did not, a chance for survival. Twenty yards out, the water changed color, indicating a drop-off. If I could get into the canoe and propel myself into deep water, I could escape Ted's reach. The gun was still a threat, but a moving target is difficult to hit, and he couldn't afford to stand on the beach taking shots at me—at least, not for long.

Staggering with fatigue, I veered toward the water. I had to flip the canoe, carry it far enough into the water to float it, get in, and launch myself outward without a single mistake. If I didn't get out far enough, the craft would stick in the sand. If I didn't keep it steady, it would tip over and fill with water. There were a dozen possible problems, but with Ted pounding closer each second, it was the best chance I had.

Reaching the canoe, I flipped it onto its keel and half-carried, half-pushed it to the water. Risking a look under my arm, I saw Ted only a few yards behind me. The lower part of his face was a mess, which was satisfying, despite my terror.

When he saw my intention he redoubled his efforts, legs pumping faster and his fists clenched in determination. Grasping the sides, I set one foot inside the craft and pushed off with my back foot as hard as I could. The impetus should have sent the canoe shooting forward, but my weight pushed the keel downward into the sand. For a moment I feared I'd remain there, six feet from shore, but I leaned forward, shifting my weight and raising the slender boat's stern. As I fought to remain balanced, the canoe floated free in the water.

My triumph was short-lived. Looking back, I saw that I was only ten feet from shore. Ted was closing, and in water this shallow he could simply wade in and catch hold of the stern. Sliding the paddle from under the seat, I dipped it in far enough for maximum thrust and pushed hard, propelling myself away from shore and into deep water.

Another glance back revealed that Ted had stopped at the water's edge. Though his nose was bleeding from the kick I'd landed, he showed no sign of giving up. Instead he pulled the gun from his waistband, set his feet shoulder-width apart, and aimed at me, bringing his free hand up to steady the weapon like they teach at the shooting range. My back muscles tensed so hard it was difficult to keep paddling. Would he dare fire at me here in the open on a sunny afternoon?

The answer was yes. In an area where hunting and target practice are normal activities, hearing shots isn't that uncommon. Zeroing in on where a noise comes from is almost impossible with one or two instances, and open water complicates things by refracting and distorting sound. Ted guessed he could get away with a shot or two, and I couldn't argue the point.

I'm not sure I heard the sound, but I felt the impact. Pain shot through me, and I lurched to one side, causing the canoe to tilt wildly. My hand went to my shoulder and found a rush of blood. I fought to keep my wits about me so I didn't tumble into Grand Traverse Bay.

For the record, wits are hard to maintain when one has a hole in her body. For a few seconds, I was unable to think anything except *I've been shot!* Instincts I'd gained canoeing the waters of the San Juan Islands helped, but still my mind screamed, *Shot! Shot! Shot!*

Forcing my way past that horrifying thought, I took stock of the situation. Light reflecting off the water was so bright it hurt. Ted was a black silhouette standing knee-deep in the water with the gun still pointed toward me. He was no doubt trying to decide whether he could afford to fire a second time and whether it was necessary. I had to convince him it wasn't.

I was thirty, maybe forty yards from shore. His choices were to swim out and get me, shoot me again, or wait and see what happened. If he did either of the first two, I'd be dead in less than a minute. My only chance was convincing him any threat I'd posed was over. My advantage was that Ted would want to believe he'd accomplished his goal and didn't need to get any wetter.

Slumping down in the canoe, I rested my head against the side and played dead. Looking out through slitted eyes, I waited, but he didn't back away. My act hadn't convinced him. Before he made a decision, I made my own—one I wasn't sure I could survive. Leaning my weight against the side, I tipped the canoe over and slid under the water.

It was cold but not unbearable. Holding the central cross bar with my undamaged arm, I stayed with the craft, though it almost shot away from the impetus of my action. Though the joint almost jerked out of its socket, I managed to surface in the convenient airspace an upside-down canoe provides.

Now all I had to do was wait until Ted was convinced I had drowned.

Chapter Thirty-three

Faye

There was no one in our hotel room. After I knocked several times, a maid came along with some towels. Smiling as if embarrassed, I told her I'd left my key inside the room. With no hesitation she used her badge to unlock the door, holding it open for me as I entered.

The room was much as I'd left it, except Retta and Bill were gone. I peered uselessly into the bathroom and even opened the louvered closet door. No one. On my second turn, I noticed a block-printed note next to the TV.

YOU KNOW THE DEAL.

It had to be either Ted or Bill who'd left it, which meant I was still expected to play the role of carefree retreat attendee. When I picked up the note, I found writing on the back side, this time in Barb's messy printing: *Exploring the landscape. Meeting a friend at six.*

I paced from the window to the door for several minutes, deciphering what that meant. "Exploring the landscape" would be searching for Retta. The kidnappers must have moved her before Barb arrived. Bill had complained he'd be missed around the inn, and Ted hadn't seemed interested in chaperoning, so they moved Retta somewhere they could lock her in and leave her unguarded. Barb was out trying to find her.

From the "meeting a friend" part, I concluded Barb had contacted the police. I hoped she'd be back soon to tell me what the plan was. Even better, she might return to say Retta was safe and we could leave this place forever.

No. If she'd found Retta, Barb would have let me know. That meant she was still looking, and I had to keep showing up at events downstairs. Bill and Ted couldn't suspect the police were on the way to arrest them.

That brought up a question. If the authorities were on the way, who would we tell them to arrest? Ted for certain and Bill too, but they weren't acting alone. Was Dina in charge or was it someone we were unaware of? My contribution would be to find out what I could about Ted and Bill's employer.

It made me antsy to sit and do nothing. I decided if I hadn't heard from Barb before I went down to dinner, I'd search the inn. There wasn't much chance Retta was locked in a closet somewhere, but it was something I could do.

Chapter Thirty-four

Retta

"Ain't nobody coming to rescue you now, Miss Love-Able Lady."

The gloating tenor of Ted's voice sent a chill down my spine. "Your friend went canoeing, and you know how dangerous them things can be. She had a bad accident."

I think he left then, but I didn't care. Leaning against that dirty, rusty old tractor, I gave in to despair and cried for a long time.

When I stopped sobbing, the sun no longer shone through the boards over the window. I went a little crazy for a while, unable to believe I could succeed but equally unable to sit and do nothing. I went over every inch of the shed again, searching places I'd already searched, knowing I wouldn't find a way out but determined to try. Soon it would be dark, and I'd be even more helpless than I was in murky daylight.

Finally I was too exhausted to continue. I retreated to my corner, telling myself I should rest so that when someone came to kill me in the morning, I could fight back. Though nothing I found felt remotely like a weapon, I settled on the crank. It was an unwieldy club due to its bent shape, but I laid it on the floor next to me. When I heard the padlock click open, I'd hurry to the door and whack Bill or Ted on the head as he came in. If they came together, I'd deal with it somehow. The fact that they'd killed Barbara made it certain Faye and I were doomed.

They killed Barbara. It was almost impossible to think that without going—as Mom would have said—"stick, stark, raving mad."

What would life be like without Barbara Ann? Of all reasons I'd miss her, the silliest came to mind: the "Correction Events" she'd begun in retirement. In the middle of the night she went out dressed in black, lugging paint cans and brushes and fixing improperly worded or punctuated signs. When I caught her at it, I'd forced her to let me come along. She was reluctant at first, and we had some minor disagreements, but overall we had fun with it.

Sometime in June we'd gone out to edit a sign on the outskirts of town that contained one of Grammar Nazi Barbara's most hated errors: misuse of *your*. Since it was election-related, I'd argued the sign was temporary and didn't merit our time. Barbara had given me a look that said she intended to fix it with or without me, so I dug out my black jeans and hoodie and rode along.

The sign said *Think about You're Vote*. Now even I know how to take a contraction apart to test correct usage. *Think about you are vote*?

Someone wasn't thinking. Sadly, he or she would still vote.

I'd stood looking at the billboard as Barbara Ann got out the correct paint colors and two brushes. "There'll be a big gap once we take out the apostrophe and the *e*," I commented. "It's going to look uneven."

"Better uneven than wrong."

That's why you can't stay mad at Barbara when she gets all fussy. It really *matters* to her.

With that thought, I recalled my sister was possibly—probably—dead, and tears filled my eyes again. Since Ted had no reason to lie, I had no reason to hope.

Chapter Thirty-five

Barb

After I tipped the canoe over, things got really fuzzy. It seemed I was both freezing and burning. I felt buoyed by the water yet squeezed by its pressure. There was darkness and there was light. My shoulder hurt like nothing I'd felt before, and the arm attached to it didn't respond to my brain's commands. Somehow I held onto the crossbar with the other hand and kept my head above the surface. I don't know how long I floated there, knowing I had to remain still and quiet but not completely able to recall why. Though I wasn't aware of it, the action of the waves pushed me shoreward, little by little. At some point I realized my foot had touched bottom.

Ducking out from under the canoe, I squinted at the beach. Ted was gone, which was a good thing, since I was incapable of doing any more to elude him. Standing was the most I might accomplish, and I reeled like a drunkard, barely able to make it to my feet. My shoulder throbbed, and it felt like someone had lit a campfire over my right eye. Putting my good hand up, I touched a lump on my forehead and heard a cry of pain. I was vaguely aware it was me who'd made the sound, and I promised myself I'd never touch that spot again, ever.

Stumbling across the beach, dripping water and blood into the bay and then onto the sand, I focused on reaching the trees. I knew I had to hide, though I could no longer articulate the threat that drove me forward. When my reaching hand touched a skinny birch, I collapsed against its trunk, my whole body one painful protest. I'd rest there for a while, just for a few minutes. Then I'd go find—what? What had I been looking for, and why? The tree's pale bark ground against my palms as my hands slid down the trunk. The sandy soil seemed to rise to meet me, hard yet soft, painful and yet so very, very restful.

Chapter Thirty-six

Faye

By six-forty I was dressed for a dinner billed in the program as formal. Retta had put the malachite-and-gold jewelry she wanted me to wear in a small fabric bag and hung it on the hanger, so I couldn't go wrong. The single jarring note was my plain black shoes, which were neither fashionable nor pretty. Retta had frowned when I packed them, saying a creamy color would go better with the dress, but I told her when you own only one pair of dress shoes, they're probably going to be black.

Aware that Retta would care what I looked like, I examined myself in the full-length mirror before leaving the room. I must admit I looked a little like a princess—maybe Fiona from *Shrek*. Along with that came the thought that in fairy tales some level of tragedy has to be endured before the good part arrives. I was definitely ready for Happily Ever After.

Dinner was a choice between pepper-crusted pork loin with apple cider gorgonzola sauce and a Rosé wine or a bacon-wrapped, stuffed chicken breast on angel-hair pasta served with Chardonnay. I went with the chicken, being unsure what gorgonzola sauce would be. Bacon I understood. My appetite wasn't good, and I struggled to appear interested in table talk about which sessions had been interesting and what life changes my companions planned as a result of their experience at the retreat. I found myself thinking the two groups—these women and the models I'd spent the afternoon with—weren't as different as they supposed. Friendship, perceptions of themselves, and concern for the future were threads that ran through every conversation. It's like Maya Angelou said, we're more alike than unalike.

When the entertainment began I excused myself, mentioning a visit to the ladies' room. The schedule included an auction for charity, some humorous prizes that promised "lots of laughs," and a funny-but-inspiring skit about the contributions older women make to their communities. I figured I had at least an hour to assure myself that Retta wasn't in the building

There was no one in the common area. Apparently even the blank-eyed perfume girl had been given the night off. I tried all the doors, poking my head into closets, storerooms, and offices. I tapped on locked doors, but only once did I get an answer. A polite clerk informed me I was in the employees-only section. Apologizing, I went on.

I didn't find Retta, but I did find Dina. The workroom she'd been given had no A/C, so she'd propped the door open with a rock. She was seated at a table with piles of clothing on both sides and her forehead damp with perspiration. The sight all but convinced me she was blameless in whatever criminal activity was going on at St. Millicent's. Who would stay up all night altering clothing for a fashion show that was only a cover for some crime?

In front of Dina was a portable sewing machine, and off to one side sat a bottle of St. Millicent's wine and a half-full glass. In a plastic chair in the far corner, Gwen was dismantling a pair of pants with a seam ripper. The machine's noise had covered the sound of my footsteps, and when she looked up and saw me in the doorway Gwen jumped, jabbing herself in the thumb. Her gasp caused Dina to notice me, and the whirr of the machine stopped. "Faye! What are you doing here?"

I couldn't very well say I was searching for my sister the kidnap victim. "I have a few minutes, so I came to see if you needed help."

She waved at the piles of clothing. "The more, the merrier."

Sitting down in the remaining chair I said, "Give me that blue frothy thing. I'll take it apart so you can sew it back together."

Still sucking her injured thumb, Gwen handed the dress across the table to Dina, who passed it to me, almost knocking her glass over as she did. I snatched the fabric out of the way, and she grinned, steadying the glass. "Oops!" Her manner told me she was tipsy, maybe more than that.

While it isn't nice to take advantage of drinkers, these were desperate times. If liquor had loosened Dina's tongue, I might learn things I wanted to know. Glancing at my watch, I guessed I had twenty minutes, maybe thirty, before the program ended and I had to return to my room.

Taking up a pair of scissors, I cut carefully along the seam line of the dress, from the armhole to a few inches below the waist. Dina returned to the piece she'd been working on, and I marveled at her coordination in light of the level of wine remaining in the bottle. Gwen's gaze met mine briefly, but without judgment. She apparently had no opinion of Dina's current condition.

They'd done an amazing job since I left at four, and there were only a half dozen items of clothing left in the to-do pile. Still, they had to press the altered pieces, reassemble the outfits, and hang them in the places designated for each model after the dining room emptied. There was plenty of work ahead.

"You probably should put the cork in that bottle," I advised as Dina refilled her glass.

She tilted her head to one side. "Would it make a difference?"

"What's going on?" I left the question wide, hoping for an answer that gave direction to the next question and the one after that.

Pulling her lips around her teeth until she looked a little like a turtle, Dina thought about it. "I called Roger and told him what I thought of his trying to sabotage my business."

"What did he say?"

"Oh, he didn't *answer*. Roger ignores any direct communication from me." She huffed in disgust. "I'll admit I haven't exactly been sweet to him lately, but then, he's never been a doting father."

"Oh."

"I left a message." She glanced at the glass but didn't take a drink. "A long one."

What I overheard on the stairs had been a monologue, not a conversation. I decided to try the direct approach. "Dina, if your father wants you to fail, why did he let you start a business in the first place?"

Her gaze slid to the wall behind me. "Let's just say he's got a lot to make up for, and I reminded him of that."

I kept my eyes on my work. "I hope that after tomorrow, he'll see that your work is worthwhile."

"With this mess?" She gestured at the piles of clothing. "Wanna-be models too short for my pants, too busty for my shirts, too clueless to tone down the brass?"

I glanced at Gwen, but she showed no resentment at being part of the "mess."

"I don't think they'll embarrass you now that they know what's expected, and you've got the alterations under control." I waited until she looked up from her work before finishing. "You just need to make sure *you're* under control when show time rolls around."

Picking up the glass, she drank the last of her wine in one gulp and set it down with a distinct *ting*. However, she did put the cork in the bottle and set it aside. "It would be great if Roger's little snitch reported the show was a success in spite of all his interference."

"You mean Honny?" Though he was certainly eccentric, the man had worked hard all afternoon. "He seemed embarrassed by the dirty tricks. I thought he helped quite a bit."

Dina grunted disdainfully. "How do you think Roger knew I'd hired professional models? How did he know to cancel my order for decent shoes?" She chuckled. "I bet Honny didn't expect his tattling to result in him schlepping all the stuff by himself this weekend."

I felt a little sorry for Honny. Trying to please two masters never works, and he'd seemed pretty good-natured about it. Still, Engel's antagonism toward his daughter struck me as odd. Was he really that petty, or was he trying to keep Dina distracted and upset?

Then it hit me: tomorrow morning, the models would be busy getting dressed and undressed. Dina would be up front, busy running things. Honny would be busy with lights, music, and whatever else needed doing. Everyone who'd come here from Detroit would be very, very busy.

Which meant that during the show, something could happen and none of them would ever know it. Something secret. Something illegal.

Knowing Engel's profession, I guessed it would be a drug deal.

"Dina, did your father seem interested in your plans for the show?"

The look she gave me was innocent. "Interested how?"

Oh, like something that warrants murder and kidnapping.

A rise in the noise level down the hall told me the evening session had ended. "I'm sorry to leave you with this, but I've got to go."

She waved away my apology. "Cecily's coming down at midnight to help us put stuff back on the hangers." As I handed her the piece I'd worked on she said, "Thanks, Faye. With all the help from you and Cecily and Gwen, we might pull this off."

"Best of luck tomorrow, or break a leg. Whatever I'm supposed to say."

She quirked a brow. "How about 'I hope your father doesn't think of another way to screw things up?' I could use a little luck in that department."

When I left she had already pulled her bottom lip under her teeth and returned to work, struggling to make the pieces she'd designed fit the women she was forced to work with. Whatever was going on at the inn tomorrow, Dina's concern was that her show would succeed.

I stopped at the front desk and told the clerk I'd misplaced my room key. After checking my I.D., she made me a new one. Joining the crowd in the common area, I moved through and headed up the stairs as if I'd been in the dining room all along.

The *Do Not Disturb* tag was still in place on the door. The room was empty, with no sign Barb had been back.

Again I considered calling the police. Bill had disabled the room phone and done away with our electronics, but I could call from downstairs and warn them to make a silent approach. Whatever Barb planned to do hadn't worked. It was time to get the local police involved.

I left the room and headed to the stairway. Scanning the lobby below, I saw that the night clerk appeared to be napping in a chair behind her desk. The common area was deserted except for one woman who sat in a chair, playing games on her phone. I recognized her as the one Barb and I had seen in the ladies' room, with tight shoes, oddly-colored hair, and a butterfly tattoo on one leg. Did she have insomnia, or were her sore feet keeping her awake?

I started downstairs just as Bill came in from outside. Spotting me, he came forward, his gaze a warning. I back-tracked to my floor, and he followed, pointing me to an alcove where we were out of sight.

"Shouldn't you be in your room?"

"What did you do with Retta?"

"She's uncomfortable, but she's safe." He made an impatient gesture. "She tried to get away, but Ted stopped that real quick."

"Did he hurt her?"

He shrugged. "She might have a bruise is all."

That relieved my mind on one sister's account. I couldn't ask about Barb, so I tried an oblique approach. "Your plan is still going forward?"

"Far's I know." The comment was an admission he wasn't in the loop. He seemed almost to regard me as sympathetic, and he went on, "Ted's all mad—something about somebody staying up all night and getting in his way."

That was interesting. "Who?"

"I don't know, but they got it worked out. I gotta use my keys to let 'em in first thing tomorrow."

"Who's 'they'?"

"Don't know."

"You're letting them in where?"

"Don't know that either." His face scrunched. "Why are you wandering around anyway?"

"Looking for you," I lied. "I wanted to know where you're keeping Retta."

"I told you she's okay." Now his mouth twisted as if he were fastening it closed. "You better get back to your room and stay there, 'cause like I said, Ted's in a bad mood. There ain't no way the cops could find your sister before he makes her dead, so it's on you what happens to her."

"No," I said angrily. "It's on Ted and it's on you, Bill. You're the ones harassing two innocent women."

He didn't like that, but he repeated his demand that I stay in my room. He even tapped a foot to show impatience as I went back down the hallway.

Back in the room, I sat on the bed and tried to make a plan. I thought Bill was fairly honest for a crook, so Retta was okay. But Barb had gone looking for Retta and then what? She might be with the "friends" her note had mentioned, but my gut said otherwise. She wouldn't leave me in the dark if she could help it. I guessed she was in trouble.

For some reason, an incident from the past came to mind. When I was in tenth grade and she was in eleventh, Barb had gotten sick. The doctor in town at the time, a young, eager type, had noted her swollen lymph nodes and overall fatigue and rushed to judgment, announcing that she might have leukemia.

Mom had freaked. Dad had gone silent, and I'd stayed awake all night, wondering what I'd do without my sister. A day later the chagrined doc admitted he'd spoken too soon. Barb had mono, the "kissing disease."

Just like back in high school, I spent the night awake, unable to stop worrying. Fully dressed in case Barb showed up, I alternated between pacing and standing at the window. Retta was somewhere "uncomfortable." Barb's whereabouts were unknown. Though I was okay, I couldn't convince myself the same was true for either of my sisters.

Chapter Thirty-seven

Barb

I woke several times, though *woke* is a relative term. During one semi-conscious moment I realized the sun was setting. The branches above me split its orange light into irregular slices. Another time I opened my eyes to darkness with a million stars peeping between the canopy of leaves overhead.

Images floated through my mind. A man with blood on his face. A door chained closed. A prissy woman barely holding her temper as she argued with me.

It didn't make sense, but it felt familiar. Recent. I listened to the sound of a light rain that pattered in the leaves above but didn't make it down to me.

It seemed there was somewhere I needed to be, but I couldn't make myself care.

When an unknown voice sounded nearby, I pulled my legs up close to my body and lay still, listening. Someone was speaking, not close but within hearing range. I heard words, but they didn't make sense. Half a conversation heard by a half-conscious brain.

"You'll move the stuff to her car while I make sure the count's right."…"Yeah, I told her eleven."…"You'll have to point her out to me."…"You said her hair is different?" ..."What's going on with those women you told me about?"…"I get that. He recognized you and then they came along."…"You're sure they were with the fed?"…"I guess if there were calls to him on their phones, they must be part of it."… "Who's this other woman you say you shot?"…"Geez, Troy, this should have been easy. Now it's all screwed up!"…"Just make sure there's nobody who can connect us to the bodies."

There was a long pause, and I thought the man had gone, but suddenly he spoke again. "He's on his way up here?"…"This is so screwed up! Let me think a minute….Okay. Tell him to meet you down here, at this little gazebo thing. Tell him whatever it takes—say the FBI is all over the inn and he can't be seen there. We don't want him to get a chance to talk to Dina."…"Okay. Tell him that and then get your guy to open that storeroom as soon as she leaves. Get the drugs out of there. Put them somewhere we can get at them once everybody's at Dina's show. I'll meet you in the parking lot after I deal with the old man."

I tried. I really tried to understand what had been said. All I ended up with was vague concepts: An old man. Drugs. Me getting a shot. That explained how lousy I felt. I was sick.

Chapter Thirty-eight

Retta

I didn't sleep, but I must have dozed. I dreamed I was back in junior high and overheard Mom and Dad talking. Because Barbara had been sleeping a lot, Mom took her to the doctor for tests. She'd been quiet when they got home, so quiet I knew there was something really wrong.

Any tween worth her salt can tell you the way to find out what your family doesn't want you to know is to eavesdrop. At nine o'clock I went upstairs like a good girl, but instead of going to bed, I slipped on my nightie and then laid down on the grate that let the heat generated in the basement furnace rise to the second floor. It was a good conduit for warmth and a great one for sound.

While Barbara slept like the dead a few feet away, I listened to Mom tell Dad and Faye that the doctor had mentioned leukemia as a possible cause of her recent symptoms. Dad's voice trembled, and Faye cried. Mom held it together, insisting the diagnosis was premature. If leukemia was a possibility, it was only one of many.

That was one of Mom's great qualities. She didn't jump to conclusions or let anyone else do it. "Face trouble by taking baby steps toward it," she often said. "There's always time to be sad later."

In that instance she'd been correct. Barb didn't have leukemia; she had mono, and we all know what that comes from.

The memory reminded me that doubting is good when things look bad. There's no sense believing the worst if there's even a tiny chance it isn't true. That's what I tried to do: believe the worst wasn't certain, at least not yet.

Chapter Thirty-nine

Faye

There was no way I felt like attending a fashion show on Sunday morning. I'd spent a miserable night in an agony of not knowing. Trying for a best-case scenario, I told myself Barb had found Retta, they'd retreated to a safe place, and the police were waiting for Ted or Bill to show up so they could arrest them. Since I didn't have access to a phone, they feared contacting me would alert the bad guys.

The end of my nightmare might be as simple as going downstairs.

Somewhere in the night I'd developed a strong urge for a cigarette. It's a terrible habit, I know, but the combination of chemicals, familiar movements, and the sense of purpose is relaxing when you don't know what else to do. And quitting, however firm your mental effort, doesn't mean your body is happy about it. I longed for the release one seven-minute smoke promised. It was a good thing there aren't cigarette machines in every corner of Michigan anymore, like there were back when I took that first puff.

I went downstairs at eight, pausing on the landing to look for Dina. She was nowhere to be seen, and I guessed she was involved in preparations for the show. The perfume girl was in her usual place, and a young woman I hadn't seen before perused the tables slowly, as if interested in everything. Not only had I not seen her before, she was too young for this group. Family, maybe, come to pick up one of the ladies when the show was finished.

Trays of pastries and urns of coffee had been set up in the common area, and early risers balanced drinks and sweet rolls awkwardly as they sat on benches or stood in corners. The notice board proclaimed sessions from eight-thirty to ten for those who hadn't yet had enough of celebrating lovable-ness.

With a cheese Danish and a cup of coffee, I took a seat on a bench when two women left to attend a session titled *Hairstyles for After Fifty*. The other was called *Dealing with Divorce*. I stayed put, pretending to read a pamphlet about charm and how it can be enhanced with the artistic application of makeup. Soon the only people in the open space were me and the long-suffering perfume girl. To be polite, I smiled. She ignored me.

Preparations for the show were in full swing, and staff members moved in and out of the dining room with purpose and a sense of excitement. I had little doubt everyone on the inn's payroll would try to get a glimpse of the excitement.

Where would the other Big Event take place, the one the fashion show would divert attention from? I doubted it would be inside, since the inn had video surveillance. If it was an exchange of drugs for money, it would take place outside the range of cameras but close enough to be convenient to both parties.

Another question came to mind: How had the drugs got here?

They couldn't have been in the boxes and trunks Honny and the valets hauled inside. We'd been through every one during rehearsal yesterday. Were they still in one of the vehicles, the property van or the limo? I didn't know what something like that would look like. How big is a drug shipment, and where does someone hide it? All I knew was what I'd seen in the movies, and even then I'd hardly paid attention.

Just then Bill came through the common area and went into the dining room with a rolled-up extension cord over his shoulder. Since the only person I knew was involved in all this was Bill, I decided to keep an eye on him. With a little fast talking, I got past the woman on guard at the dining room door and entered the busy world of an impending fashion show.

Dina was there, looking fresh despite her late night. She was explaining to Bill how she wanted lights set up behind the panels that closed off the models' area. When he turned and saw me his face reddened, but his eyes warned me to keep quiet.

"I came to see if you need help," I told Dina.

"That's great, Faye, especially since Honny's run off."

"What? Where did he go?"

She looked disgusted. "He left a note: *Sorry, girl, but your dad called me back to the city. You're on your own.* Like the hound he is, Honny went loping off to do his master's bidding." As I absorbed that news, she went on, "Cecily's organizing the girls, and my friend here is finishing the things Honny was supposed to get done this morning."

"I can't believe your father would pull your only helper on the day of the show."

"Honestly, I didn't think even he would sink that low." Her voice wavered, and I sensed Dina knew exactly what her father was. She'd probably been ashamed of him her whole life. Now she was more angry than ashamed.

Should I tell her what I knew? Bill met my gaze, and I saw him shake his head as if he'd heard my thought. He was reminding me my sister's life depended on my silence.

I still had the hope—though I had to hang onto it with all my might—that Barb was working somewhere in secret to find and release Retta. As long as we were all in a room together, none of us was at physical risk, at least as far as I could tell.

"What do you want me to do?"

"Can you cover the lights and sound—the jobs Honny was supposed to do? You've seen the show and know how it will go."

My instinct was to say no, I couldn't handle it, but Dina needed help, and she was right. I was the only one free of other duties, the only one who knew the agenda. I nodded agreement, and soon I was being tutored by Bill, learning where the light switches were and how the music system worked.

At 10:15 we had five minutes before the doors opened and allowed the guests in. The show was paired with a champagne brunch, the final meal of the retreat, so one side of the room crawled with waiters setting out food and lighting little warming pans. Bill was taping down the cords so no one tripped over them. Huddled in their enclosure, the models chatted nervously, unsure of themselves now the time was near.

"I hope I don't screw up again," Candice said. Her eyes were clearer today, and she seemed to know where she was and what was going on. That was good.

"What if we get jammed up in the dressing room and can't find our stuff?" Bibi asked. Her first outfit, a navy-and-white dress, looked good on her. When no one answered, she repeated the question.

"You'll do fine," Cecily assured her. "I'll keep things moving."

Responding to her confident tone, the others settled down a little. Cecily gave me a glance that hinted she wasn't as sure of things as she pretended, but despite everyone's concerns, the models looked good. I thought overall they'd be okay.

For some reason we hadn't been able to find the platform that was supposed to fit against the dais, creating a runway the models could use to make their turns close to the crowd. The speculation was that Honny had stored it somewhere and forgotten to tell someone. "We can do without it," Dina announced, "but I know it was packed in the van with the rest of the stuff."

"What did it look like?" I asked.

"Like a folding table, only thicker. You open it up, adjust the legs to whatever height you need, and set it in place."

"Maybe someone thought it belonged to the inn and stuck it in a storeroom." Dina shrugged, and we dropped the subject. We simply didn't have time to go searching for a non-essential, though handy, bit of equipment.

I did manage to address personal concerns at one point. Dina went off to see to something, leaving Bill and me alone for a moment. Grabbing his arm I asked, "When are you going to let my sister go?" I almost made it plural, but if he didn't know Barb was here, he wasn't going to hear it from me.

"Keep doing what you're told. Ted's gonna take care of it soon."

"When?"

"When this is over."

"And what is 'this'?"

He hung his head. "I don't know exactly, but don't screw it up, or things ain't gonna turn out good for any of us."

It should have been satisfying to see Bill admit he was in over his head. At that moment in time, feeling satisfaction was as impossible for me as a starting pitcher job with the Detroit Tigers.

A noise from the kitchen caught my attention, and Gail and Dail came into the room, carrying what had to be the missing platform.

"Where did you find that?" Dina asked.

"By the back door," Dail answered. "We went out for a smoke and there it was."

"You two are stars in my book." Dina told them. "Thank you, thank you!" It was the first time I'd seen genuine smiles on the twins' faces, and I realized that everyone likes appreciation from the boss, even Biker Babes.

Bill quickly set the platform in place, and Dina and I covered it with white drapery. As soon as that was finished, Dina gave the signal to open the doors, and attendees flooded in, eager for the elegant brunch and the show that would end the retreat. Dina was already in place near the podium, and her gaze met mine for a second, signaling she was ready. I sent her a smile for luck.

One of the women I'd had dinner with on Friday, a square-jawed sort with a body to match, noticed me. "Is your sister still laid up?"

"I'm afraid so."

"Come and sit with us," she urged, gesturing at her companions, who were saving seats for themselves by leaning the folded chairs against the table.

"Thanks for asking, but I volunteered to help out with the show."

"Ooh," she said. "Did you get to meet the models?"

"Um, yes."

She eyed the curtained area. "It must be nice. They get to wear beautiful clothes and all they have to do is walk a little and then stand still."

I saw modeling differently. Judged for looks alone. Forced to smile and pretend you're not cold, bored, and uncomfortable. Unable to eat a single cookie without worrying about gaining weight. It wasn't my idea of an easy job. Rather than argue, I fell back on my mother's favorite comment when she couldn't agree but didn't want to be disagreeable. "I'm sure it's interesting."

The woman went off to join her friends at the buffet tables, while I peeped in at the models to see if they needed anything. Cecily was ready, and she was explaining something to Pixi, who looked confused, as usual. Li was covering the tattoos on Gail's arms with makeup. She was less intimidating without multiple strands of barbed wire on each arm.

Taken as a group and without considering what they'd been doing two nights ago at Engel's club, the women I saw resembled models I'd seen on TV, with a couple of obvious exceptions. Most models aren't under five feet tall, but Dina had cut large chunks off the legs of the pants now worn by the three Asian girls. Plenny appeared to have two helium balloons under her shirt, and Bibi's hair had a greenish tint the brown rinse hadn't been able to hide. "Smile and keep it moving, girls," I heard Cecily advise. "Like they say, razzle-dazzle 'em."

I'd always thought of brunch as a light meal, but that wasn't true at Love-Able Ladies. Stations along one whole wall offered omelets, French toast on a stick, and fancy fruit cups. Of course there was wine. The guests filled their plates as they chatted, sneaking peeks at where the models waited behind the curtain. The roll and coffee I'd had earlier settled at the base of my stomach like wet sand, so while the food looked incredible, I had no desire to eat.

After one last check with Cecily, I took my place at the bank of lights where Honny should have been. Dina nodded and I flashed the lights, signaling we were ready to begin. When the last guest had taken her seat, I dimmed the lights at the back three-quarters of the room, focusing attention at the front.

Dina introduced herself and welcomed the audience to her mini-reveal, speaking with dignity, professionalism, and warmth. It was impossible for the listeners to tell what a mess the last twenty-four hours had been like for her. I hoped they wouldn't be able to tell when the models came out.

Another nod from Dina, and I turned on the music she'd chosen. I recognized the first one, an instrumental version of "Just an Old-fashioned Love Song." There was a rustle as the audience turned to look at Cecily, and they followed with their eyes as she glided to the front.

She looked fabulous.

Though she wore the typical model's stare, before she turned to step onto the dais Cecily sent me the slightest of winks. Mounting the steps gracefully, she reached the center, turned onto the runway, and came forward, where she pivoted so everyone in the room could see her from all angles. Someone started clapping, and everyone joined in.

Never changing her expression, Cecily returned to the dais and exited on the opposite side.

Everyone clapped again.

As Cecily disappeared into the darkness on the right-hand side, Dail came up the center aisle. I almost didn't recognize her, though her less-than-light footsteps gave her away. By some miracle she appeared neither belligerent nor angry, and the outfit we'd chosen for her softened her square form and made her seem almost feminine. Dail's turns were less impressive than Cecily's had been, but she managed to get through her walk without a mistake. Again the audience clapped appreciatively.

As the Everly Brothers' "That's Old-fashioned" played in the background, Pixi came out, then Candice, who looked like someone's kid sister ready for her first formal dance. The others followed in turn as the song switched to Merle Haggard's "Old Fashioned Love." Some did beautifully, others were passable. I was amazed by the effect the clothing had on their attitudes. Though Jin giggled once as she left the dais, she was lovely in shimmering violet. Plenny, who came next, still resembled a cheerleader performing for the varsity team, but she managed to keep her posturing to acceptable levels.

As I watched the final round, I became acutely aware of the passage of time. Somewhere nearby a crime was taking place, and Honny's abrupt departure meant he was involved, doing as Roger Engel had told him to. The question that bothered me was what would happen afterward. Would he tell Ted to let Retta go? Would he leave her locked in whatever place she was being held so we could find her once they were gone? I looked around to see where Bill was, but he had disappeared while I was taken up with my duties.

I was furious with myself. How had I let him slip away? After the last model glided along her pathway to the strains of B. J. Thomas' "Whatever Happened to Old Fashioned Love?" I turned the lights back on, breaking the spell the show had cast on the guests. Surrounded by women who surged forward to congratulate her, Dina didn't see me slip out of the room.

Chapter Forty

Retta

It's terrible when your mind won't let a thought go, though there's not a thing you can do to change what's happening or what happened. All night long I worried about my sisters. Though I tried to keep in mind I was next if I didn't prepare, I couldn't stop thinking about Barbara. If she was dead, it was my fault for insisting on taking this dumb case on in the first place.

Of course I thought about Styx too. If I never returned, my dog wouldn't understand where I'd gone or why I'd left him. He'd be very sad, and he'd probably wait at the end of the driveway like one of those dogs you read about—

In the middle of all that, my brain did what brains do when you stop trying to force a memory. As if he stood over me at that very moment, I heard Dad's voice inside my head. "Go to North Carolina." That was the mnemonic for starting the tractor. <u>GtNC</u> stood for *gas, throttle, neutral, choke.* Those were the steps; that was the order. After that you went to the front and cranked hard.

I jumped up, eager to try the newly-recalled information. As I did, I heard voices approaching the shed. Bill and Ted. I crept close to the door to listen.

"—let her go?" Bill was asking.

"When we're ready to take off," Ted replied. I heard the clink of metal as he added, "Here, let me hold that while you open the lock."

"I guess I should pack some things—Hey!" Bill's voice registered surprise. I heard, "Uh!" and no more.

Bill wasn't leaving with Ted. He would be yet another casualty of the weekend.

The sounds that followed were hard to interpret, but I guessed Bill was being set up. He'd take the blame for all the deaths this weekend: Chet Auburn, Barbara Ann, and me, no doubt. But in an ending worthy of an Ambrose Bierce story, Bill would die too, probably in an "accident" that would leave no way to question him about why we'd died and how it was done. The cases would close, and people would say to each other, "Who knew what kind of monster was hiding inside an apparently normal man's mind?"

A muffled groan sounded outside, telling me Bill wasn't dead yet. I had to get to him before Ted finished what he'd started. Stepping to the tractor I turned the on switch, and, repeating, "Go to North Carolina" in my head, approached the tractor's left side and turned on the gas. That was the step I'd forgotten earlier, and leaving it out had made everything else I tried useless. Once I remembered there *was* a gas switch, it was easy to find. Moving to the dashboard, I set the throttle about a third of the way up and reached over to put the gearshift in neutral. Going back to the side, I pulled the choke out an inch to let gas enter the carburetor. Once I turned the crank, I'd hurry back and close it so the engine didn't get too much fuel and die. It was a delicate balance, but I felt confident. Barbara believed I could do it, and Dad had taught me how.

I left the seat, lifted the crank from the toolbox behind it, and went to the front. As soon as I fired up the tractor engine Ted would know it, so I had to move quickly.

Setting the crank into its hole at the front of the tractor as quietly as possible, I took a deep breath, set my feet, and cranked hard. My shoulder wasn't happy with yet another attempt, but this time my ears were rewarded with the *chug-chug-ROAR* of the engine coming to life.

I hurried to the back, closing the choke on the way, and hefted myself into the tractor seat. The engine made an odd hiccup every once in a while that told me it wasn't in the best state of repair. Would it go when I put it into gear, or would it cough to a stop? Only one way to find out.

Again it was as if Dad spoke to me: *First gear is up and to the left.* Muscle memory told me the pedal on the left was the clutch. I tried it and felt the gears engage. Grabbing the rubber-coated steering wheel with both hands, I lifted my foot and said a little prayer.

The big machine started forward with a lurch that rocked me back in the seat, but it went. Tractors have no regard for barriers, and the nails that held the metal hinge to the wooden door separated with a screech of protest. One door burst off its hinges; the other was bumped aside by the front wheel of my mighty steed.

Ted crouched over Bill's prone body, and he looked up at me in surprise as my iron horse bore down on him. He had a decision to make. If he stayed where he was, I'd run him over. He might take his gun out and shoot me, but that wouldn't stop the tractor. The smartest thing he could do was run. That's what Ted did.

Pulling the gearshift into neutral, I set the brake and got down to see if Bill was still breathing. He was. In fact, he opened his eyes and looked at me—at least one of his eyes did. Though definitely loopy, he seemed to understand he'd been had. "Tried to kill me."

"I warned you." Not a nice thing to tell him at that point, but I wasn't sure he was processing the spoken word anyway. "Come on, Bill. We have to get you to a doctor."

"Creighton," he mumbled. "Call me Cray."

"All right, Cray. Can you stand?" He did, with a lot of help from me. I was pretty sure he couldn't walk far, and certainly not the distance to the inn. "Get up on the tractor."

"What?"

"The tractor. Can you get up there?" I led him to the back and pointed at the C-shaped hitch bar. "Use that for a step, and pull yourself up by holding onto the seat."

I demonstrated, climbing up then back down. He nodded solemnly, though I could tell he wasn't quite with me. "I can do that."

He tried twice unsuccessfully, losing his hold on the seat the first time and failing to lift himself high enough to reach the platform the second. In the end I put a shoulder into his bum and boosted him in an upward direction. It wasn't pretty, but eventually he landed in the metal seat, reeling like a kid just off the Tilt-a-Whirl. I set one of his hands on the left fender and the other on the right. "Hang on," I ordered. He did.

That left the question of how I was going to drive. Tractors aren't set up so a person—at least a petite person with short arms, can drive from anywhere but the seat. There was only one way to do it, and though I shuddered at the thought, it's like they say, necessity is the mother of invention. Climbing up to the platform, I stepped in front of him and sat down on his lap. Immediately he wrapped his arms around my waist, but I peeled them off and set his hands back on the fenders. "Stay like that. We're going to get you some help, understand?"

Bill laid his face against the back of my neck. "Wahoo."

Chapter Forty-one

Faye

As I left the dining room, I saw that the help had set various kinds of wine on the table so we could purchase some to take home. Several women stood reading labels, some with a bottle in each hand, frowning as they tried to choose. Threading my way among them, I headed up the staircase to the room, hoping to find a sister or two there.

The place was just as I'd left it, and I faced the fact that something had gone terribly wrong. I should have called the police last night, as soon as it became clear that Barb wasn't coming back. I should have told Dina there was a crime happening during her show. I should have followed Bill when he left the dining room. I'd failed one sister while trying to save the other, and they both might pay for my indecision. Suddenly weak with self-loathing, I sat on the bed and wished I'd never heard of St. Millicent's. I wished I were anywhere but here.

Giving in to despair is for me a typical but usually brief response to stress. Though I'm aware I tend to blame myself too much when things go wrong, I need to let feelings of guilt and remorse wash over me for a few minutes before I can put things into perspective and move on. There are even articles that say it can be good for you, as long as you limit the time you allow yourself to spend doing it.

After my sense of failure abated somewhat, I was able to make a decision. I would go back downstairs, ask to use a house phone, and call Barb's cell. If she didn't answer, I'd call the local police. Maybe they could stop Bill, Ted, and Honny before they left. Even if—and I had to bite my lip as the thought came to me—even if things had gone wrong for my sisters, I needed to *do* something instead of pretending everything was okay, as I'd been forced to do all weekend.

I stood up. Time to stop wallowing and take action.

When I opened the door, the perfume girl stood there, her hand raised to knock. She wore another girlish outfit, short skirt, knee socks, and a sweater so tight it looked like it belonged to her younger sister. Her eyes met mine, and in their depths I read two things. First, she was the one who'd been watching me all weekend. Second, her dead expression didn't come from boredom. It came from a lack of any sort of genuine human emotion.

"Back inside." She raised the hand that had been concealed in the pleats of her skirt to show me a wicked-looking knife. I stared at it, almost able to feel it slicing into my flesh. I imagined her calmly wiping the blade on my sleeve after she'd killed me. Sometimes you just know things about people.

Farther down the hallway a door slammed, and three women came toward us. The girl returned the weapon to her side. "Inside," she said again, more urgently this time.

A braver person might have refused, but the imminent threat of being stabbed was too real for me. I obeyed. Following me into the room, she kicked the door closed with her foot. I heard the women in the hall exchanging goodbyes and promises to stay in touch.

Somehow I knew I wasn't going to be keeping in touch with anyone anymore. Of all the crimes committed at St. Millicent's this weekend, my death was going to be the last one. There would be no one left alive to say what had happened or who had been involved.

Facing a weapon in the hands of someone who fully intends to use it is one of the scariest things a person can do. I'd faced a gun before, but for me a knife was worse. Imagining what it would do to me, wondering how long it would take me to die, I felt my courage trickle away like raindrops on a tree branch. I retreated from the blade until the backs of my legs touched the bed then sidled around it to the far side, putting myself as far from it as possible.

Weird things ran through my head. I thought of Buddy. He'd be all right if I died, because Dale would see to his needs. Still, it was sad to think of him roaming the house and whining, wondering why I'd abandoned him. And Dale. Would he—?

"Don't yell," the girl said. "You'll be dead before anyone can get up here to help you."

I didn't have an answer for that, but for some reason her words helped me pull myself together. Putting together all my guesses I asked, "Are you part of the drug deal that took place today?"

She snickered. "We didn't come up here to sell Avon."

"So you work for Roger Engel."

"Roger?" She made a rude sound. "We got our own thing going."

That sent my thoughts in a different direction. After a few seconds of re-evaluating I said. "You and Honny are double-crossing Engel."

Her lips formed what I figured was for her a smile. "Honny, yeah, and Troy and me. I'm Troy's girl."

I guessed Troy was the man I knew as Ted. "That sounds dangerous to me."

"We got it all figured out." She listened for a moment. The three women in the hall were still out there talking, which meant she couldn't kill me yet. "Engel had a shipment come in that's supposed to go to his people. When we found out about the show this weekend, Honny made his own deal with a woman up here. On Monday Roger will find out his drugs are missing, but we'll be gone by then with a million bucks."

"What about Dina—?"

She laughed aloud. "Dina's clueless. She never liked her dad much, but Honny plays them against each other so they never really talk."

If a person can feel better when she's about to be murdered, the news that I hadn't been wrong about Dina helped a little.

Something clicked into place in my head. "Honny brought the drugs here in the platform."

"A million-dollar prize inside the box." She raised a drawn-on eyebrow. "Better than Cracker Jacks."

"He couldn't get at them because Dina worked all night on the clothes."

"Yeah. It slowed us up a little, but we handled it."

"What about my sisters?"

"The one who drowned, or the one that got strangled by the crazy inn employee?" The same sickly smile appeared. "That crazy maintenance man murdered the FBI guy too. Ain't that weird?"

I was struck silent, but she didn't seem to notice. The voices in the hallway finally faded as the women finished their goodbyes and parted company. The perfume girl came toward me. "If you holler now, no one will hear you. It's time to get back on schedule."

That's what my death would be to this woman—an item to be ticked off on a to-do list. As she came around the bed, I realized I'd boxed myself in. I had nowhere to go. I knew the window didn't open, and even if it did, dropping twenty feet onto concrete pool area would probably result in serious injury. The bed was on my left and the wall was behind me. If I launched myself over the bed, could I move fast enough to escape? The knife blade looked so sharp, so deadly.

A knock on the door made me jump. "Faye?" a familiar voice called. "They said you hadn't checked out yet."

The perfume girl stopped, her expression frustrated. Would she simply ignore my visitor and hope she went away?

"Faye, are you okay?" It was Dina, and she sounded worried. My knife-wielding guest rolled her eyes in frustration.

Three loud knocks. "Faye?"

With an irritated gesture, the woman indicated I should answer the door. She stepped back so I could get past her then followed me, positioning herself in a spot where she couldn't be seen from the hallway. The knife stayed at my back, and though she didn't actually touch me with it, the sensation of sharp metal at the center of my spine was all too real.

I opened the door to find Dina holding a vase of flowers and smiling broadly. "I brought these as a token of my gratitude."

I looked at her in confusion. The flowers she carried were a centerpiece that had sat on a table in the hallway all weekend. Had she come to thank me with stolen blooms and an institutional vase?

Dina was staring at me intently, and I read a message in her gaze. "Why, that's so nice of you," I said, and her eyes approved.

"Now where I can set them down?" she said, taking a step forward.

Behind me the perfume girl shifted, and I guessed the knife had slipped out of sight. Dina frowned when she saw her. "Gretchen?"

"I came to thank her too," the woman said weakly. "I-uh-I didn't think you'd have time with all the stuff you had to do."

Dina nodded as if that were a perfectly acceptable explanation. "These are kind of heavy. Where do you want them?"

"Um, over there." I pointed at the dresser, aware this was my chance to live through the day. I had to disarm the perfume girl without getting either Dina or myself hurt or killed.

Dina was way ahead of me. As she passed between me and Gretchen, she tilted the vase, spilling water down the front of Gretchen's shirt. When Gretchen stepped back with a gasp, Dina reached out her free hand and shoved her hard, knocking her onto the bed. Using the vase as a weapon she struck at the knife, which went flying into a corner. The vase dropped to the floor with a crash as Dina launched herself at Gretchen and pinned her to the bed.

She didn't give up easily. Raising her legs like a Big Time Wrestler, Gretchen tried to twist out from under Dina. She didn't succeed on the first try, but when she did it again, Dina slid off to one side. That was when I realized I should be helping. Stepping onto the bed, I sat down on Gretchen's torso, squashing her into the mattress and rendering her incapable of drawing enough breath to keep fighting.

"Tell me what's going on," Dina demanded once the wriggling stopped and our captive contented herself with muttering curse words.

"You just saved my life."

She nodded. "I thought you were in trouble." Her expression turned bleak. "This has something to do with my father, doesn't it?"

"I'm afraid so."

Taking off the scarf she wore, Dina tied one end tightly around Gretchen's wrist while I held it still. "I really was coming to thank you. Then I saw her at your door." Together we forced Gretchen onto her stomach and twisted her hands behind her so Dina could tie the second wrist to the first. Gretchen had gone silent, though she glared at us over her shoulder. "I couldn't figure out why she'd be going to your room, but she's one of Honny's creatures, and after this morning I started wondering what he was up to. By listening at the door, I heard enough to conclude you needed help."

"I certainly did," I agreed. "Now if you'll lend me your phone, it's time we called the police."

Chapter Forty-two

Barb

I woke again to the sound of voices—two this time. I thought I was at home, in my bedroom, and my father was talking downstairs. He seemed worried about me. *Will I have to miss school?* Make-up work was the worst.

"I thought you'd take care of my girl," Dad was saying.

Was the doctor here—at the house? Or was I in the hospital?

I really did feel terrible. It might have helped to move to a more comfortable position, but I couldn't make my limbs obey. Raising my head a little, I tried to open my eyes.

That made everything hurt worse.

"I did what I thought was right," another man said.

"You're up to something," Dad said. Only it wasn't Dad. This voice was harder, harsher. I didn't know him. I tried to lift my head and look, but again, it hurt too much.

"You gotta believe me—" the second man began.

"I believed you for too long," the kind-of-like-Dad man interrupted. "Last night after I got her message, I did some investigating. You're trying to screw me, Honey." Did he just call another man "Honey"?

"That's not true." The tone shifted from conciliatory to gloating. "I did screw you." A sound followed that resembled a fist smacked twice into a palm. Someone grunted in surprise. No one spoke again. More sounds followed, soft grunts of exertion and a splash as something hit water.

Water? That meant I was neither at home on the farm nor in a hospital.

An image of a dog came to mind. It wasn't the old collie we'd had on the farm, but a squat, homely mutt with intelligent eyes who'd tried to tell me something. *Animals sense things people don't,* he seemed to say. *You should have paid better attention to my warning.*

It was too much to think about, and I surrendered again to the state of not thinking.

Chapter Forty-three

Faye

Using Dina's phone, I called 9-1-1 and explained there was an emergency at St. Millicent's Inn. Leaving Dina to guard Gretchen, I went down to meet the police when they arrived. I was cautious, fearing I'd run into Bill or Ted lurking somewhere, ready to do me harm.

Had they already killed my sisters? I had to believe I still had time to save them.

Through the wide windows of the front wall, I saw that most of the retreat guests were either gone or in the parking lot, preparing for departure. The only person in the common area was Angel, who sensed immediately that something was wrong. "Are you all right, dear?"

"There's been at least one murder," I told her. "I've called the police. Dina Engel has one of the killers under guard in my room."

Her eyes and mouth rounded in surprise, and she stuttered, "Wh-wh-wh-?" I went on, eager to get outside, but I heard her say as I went, "There can't be any of our ladies involved. We're a completely non-violent group."

Leaving the cool inn for the hot sidewalk, I listened for sirens. What I heard instead was the troubled sound of an engine in dire need of a tune-up. It was coming from behind the inn, and as I turned, relief flooded my heart at an unexpected—slightly unbelievable—sight.

Across the parking lot came an old Farmall tractor, its chugging motion signaling sediment in the gas. Retta was in the driver's seat, her hands tight on the wheel. Under her sat Bill, his forehead streaked with blood. He wore a faint grin, and he held tightly to Retta's waist, apparently to keep himself upright.

She waved when she saw me, stopped the machine with an abrupt jerk, and shut off the engine. The silence was momentarily deafening.

"Have you seen Barbara Ann?" she called.

"I was hoping she was with you."

A look of foreboding crossed her face as she dismounted, leaving Bill where he was. He listed to one side without her to steady him, but Retta pinched his elbow and he rallied somewhat, leaning his chin against the steering wheel for balance.

Retta looked as un-Retta-like as I'd ever seen her: dirty clothes, unkempt hair, and a grimy face that revealed tracks of tears. We hurried to each other and hugged for a long time. "Barb found me, but then that awful Ted came along," she said in my ear. "I don't know what happened after that." Gretchen's taunt came to mind. One of my sisters had drowned, she said, the other had been strangled.

Sirens sounded then, and we turned to see two county cars and an ambulance turning into the drive.

Retta met the EMTs and led them to where Bill waited, still half out of it. While she explained what had happened to him, I stepped forward to identify myself to the deputies. "You have to arrange a search," I told them. "Our other sister is missing."

Immediately one deputy took out his phone and relayed the information I provided: when I'd last seen Barb, where she might have gone, and her physical description. When he ended the call he said, "We'll have help up here in no time, ma'am. Now can you give me a better idea of what's going on?"

"First we should go relieve Ms. Engel of her prisoner." Explaining as we went, I led him and another deputy upstairs to my hotel room. There they took charge of a sulky Gretchen, replacing Dina's scarf with handcuffs before marching her out of the inn between them. Dina and I trailed behind them like bridal attendants who don't quite know what comes next.

Once Gretchen was locked in the back seat of a county car, the deputy in charge, whose name was Barrett, took out his note pad. "I'd like to get a few things on record now, and we'll fill in the details later."

I repeated my plea for a search, and he assured me it was being organized. "We'll find your sister, but I need to know what's going on here. You said that woman tried to kill you?"

"Apparently she's part of a group that brought a bunch of drugs up here to sell."

That caught Deputy Barrett's interest. "Can we start at the beginning?"

Dina started an account, and I soon learned she'd pumped information out of Gretchen while they were alone upstairs. "Honny Bellows used my show as cover for a drug sale."

"He had the drugs hidden in the fashion show stuff?" I asked.

"Exactly." Dina turned to Barrett, her smile grim. "My father assigned Honny to help me. He kept making changes to my plans, and he said my father ordered them. Really, he was doing it to keep me distracted."

It was interesting to me that Engel had become "my father" sometime in the last few hours.

"Last night I called home to hash things out. I got no answer, so I left a message explaining how upset I was about the way my father had chipped away at my success." She took out her phone and showed it to the deputy. "After the show today, I saw that I had a text from him. He had no idea what I was talking about."

"He's on his way up here to look into it," Barrett said as he scanned the message. He frowned. "This was sent ten hours ago. He should be here by now."

I was struggling to keep up. "Your father didn't know about the canceled contract with the modeling agency?"

"Or the shoes or the lack of help with setup," Dina replied. "It was all Honny's doing." Frowning, she added, "I don't doubt he pocketed the difference between what Roger okayed and what he actually paid."

I'd been right to think Dina's problems were meant to be distractions, but wrong about who'd planned them.

"The guy doesn't sound very trustworthy," Barrett commented.

Dina looked down at her hands. "I blamed my father for so many things, and I was ready to believe the worst…" After a moment she cleared her throat and returned to facts. "Honny disappeared this morning, but I had the show to do. Again he blamed my father, and I accepted that as the truth, at least until I saw that message."

"Actually, Honny was finalizing a deal he'd made without Mr. Engel's knowledge." I was catching on.

Barrett gestured at Gretchen. "Why did she try to harm Mrs. Burner?"

"Murder is the word." Dina smiled grimly. "Faye, she says you saw them kill someone."

Barrett looked at me. "Is that right?"

"Well, close. We came along just afterward. The killer wanted my sister and me dead so we couldn't describe him to the police."

"But they couldn't afford a fuss until the deal was made, so they forced Faye to pretend things were okay by holding her sister hostage." Dina glanced at Gretchen. "She told me everything once I reminded her there are worse things than going to jail."

Barrett didn't pick up on that, but I did. Whatever Dina wanted to believe about her father, she sensed how ruthless he could be. She'd threatened Gretchen with his wrath, and Gretchen had spilled her guts.

Our poor deputy was barely keeping up. "So there are two criminals at large in the area," he said, glancing around the property. "One of them killed someone, and they both are selling drugs."

"Yes," Dina said. "Troy is the killer, but I don't know his last name. He's Gretchen's boyfriend, and he's been up here for several days, setting things up for Honny. They were waiting for their buyer to get the money together, which she did this morning."

"Troy." We described him, and Barrett wrote it down. "And who's that?" He gestured at Bill, who was being loaded into the ambulance.

Dina shrugged. "I don't know that guy."

"He was low-level help," I supplied. "I don't think he knew he was into something this big."

Shifting his feet, Barrett wrote for some time before saying, "And these people brought illegal drugs to Leelanau County."

"Cocaine, and a lot of it," Dina supplied. "It was hidden in a platform we used for a runway, which was stored with my equipment." She turned to me, adding, "When I went up to my room to change for the show, Gretchen and Troy took the drugs out and hid them in the van, but it was so close to show time when they got done they couldn't put the platform back inside without being seen."

"Which is why Dail and Gail found it outside the kitchen door."

Barrett wasn't following our sidebar conversation, and he prompted, "The drug deal?"

Dina nodded. "Troy arranged it with some local woman who attended the retreat like a regular guest. After they did whatever maneuvering it takes for one criminal to trust another, they agreed to exchange the drugs for cash while everyone was inside watching the show."

"Not a bad idea," Barrett acknowledged. "Who'd suspect a drug deal at an event like this?"

Retta joined us, and I introduced her to Dina and Barrett, who asked, "Any idea where Honny Bellows and Troy Whoever are now?"

"Gretchen says Troy had some things to clear up," Dina replied.

"Like killing me and Bill." Retta rolled her eyes. "That didn't go so well."

"Honny's supposed to meet Gretchen and Troy in Traverse City this afternoon, but she didn't know exactly where."

"Maybe the models know something," I suggested.

Barrett called to another officer. "Weisnewski, talk to those women over by the limo and see what they know about where Honny Bellows might be." Demonstrating wisdom beyond his years he added, "Take Ms. Engel along with you. They'll tell her things they won't tell you."

Chapter Forty-four

Retta

The Leelanau County sheriff's men took charge of the woman Faye identified as Gretchen. The EMTs helped poor Bill into the ambulance, but I'm not sure he understood he was under arrest. The officers proceeded on the assumption he might be faking nuttiness in order to escape. I could have told them Bill (or Cray, as I now knew him) was a little nutty to begin with, but I supposed it didn't matter. Either way, he was in a lot of trouble.

I managed to convince a young EMT that I was fine despite a slightly black eye from when Ted stopped my escape. I answered questions about who was the President and what year it was. When they let me go, I went to where Faye was talking to the deputy in charge. Walking away from them with a female deputy was a woman I soon learned was Dina Engel.

"I think she's telling the truth as she knows it," Faye was saying as I approached. To me she said, "Deputy Barrett is trying to figure out if Dina is part of whatever went on here. Did you hear Bill or Ted say anything that would indicate she is?"

When I shook my head Faye said, "I think Dina came here to put on a fashion show. I thought at first her father was using the event to cover a drug sale, but now it appears the deal was arranged by Dina's assistant, Honny Bellows."

"He stole the drugs from his boss? He's either very brave or very dumb." Apparently Faye had told the deputy who Roger Engel was.

"Gretchen claimed they'd have a million dollars and a head start."

"A million?" Barrett whistled softly. "I can only think of three people around here who could afford a buy that big." Rolling his shoulders he added, "Lots of times we know who the dealers are, but we can't prove it."

"From what I've read, that's exactly how Engel has stayed in business all these years," I said. "Who's your main suspect?"

Barrett got all official. "I can't say, ma'am. It wouldn't be professional."

"In the first place," I informed him, "we're private detectives working with the FBI." He looked slightly impressed but mostly doubtful. "In the second place, a name wouldn't mean a thing to us. I just wondered if one of the three would be a woman in her fifties."

He looked surprised. "Well, yes, as a matter of fact. The last time I saw her, she had her hair dyed black on top and purple underneath."

"She's here," Faye said. "I spoke to her yesterday, and I saw her again last night in the common area. Now that I think of it, she might have been waiting for someone."

After Barrett called down to Traverse City to get a warrant for the arrest of the woman who now had the cocaine, I sketched the scenario, as much for myself as for the others. "Your local drug dealer came on Friday as a retreat guest. The guy who called himself Ted rode up with his girlfriend—her." I pointed at the girl in the squad car. "They met with the buyer and set things up for Sunday morning. Then Ted saw Agent Auburn, recognized him, and decided he had to be eliminated."

"If the agent was investigating Engel," Faye said, "he'd have seen photos of the people who work for him."

"Right. Now Ted paid Bill—the guy in the ambulance over there— to let him stay at his place to avoid Dina or the models seeing him. His name is Cray, and he works here at St. Millicent's, so he had keys to the places they needed to get into."

"Their first problem came when Auburn recognized them," Faye said. "Their second was that we happened along before they could get rid of the body."

"Cray wasn't really in on the murder," I told the deputy. "He thought he was helping with some minor crime like burglary."

Barrett wasn't sympathetic. "But he didn't flinch when a federal agent got killed."

"Well, he did flinch," I said, but it was a moot point. Cray was in a lot of trouble, and there was nothing I could do to save him.

An EMT approached. "Deputy? We're ready to transport."

"Okay," Barrett replied. Turning to us he said, "Excuse me for a minute. I want to make sure my guy reads the suspect his rights a second time at the hospital, so nobody can say later he was unable to understand them."

When the ambulance pulled away a few minutes later, a car turned into the drive. A man and a woman sat in the front seat and a second man slumped in the back. I recognized the man I knew as Ted, though he didn't look nearly as confident as when I'd last seen him. The creases along his mouth were caked with dirt, and he'd turned his shirt inside out in a vain attempt to hide bloodstains there. His appearance made me a little glad and a lot sad. Barbara Ann had certainly put up a fight, and she'd have been pleased to see the swollen bump that indicated her killer's nose was broken. I hoped he never breathed easily again.

The man and woman were FBI agents, Terry Draco and Tonya Holden, and they'd responded to Barbara's call for help. "We waited at the meeting place last night, but she didn't show," Agent Holden told us when the introductions and badge-flipping were done. "We figured she ran into trouble. Terry dropped me off up here, but things seemed normal. No one I spoke to had ever heard of Barbara Evans. We went to your room, but it was empty. We decided it was best not to announce our presence, since Ms. Evans said Mrs. Stilson was in danger."

My heart sank a little as she said that. I was okay, but where was Barbara Ann? Holden finished, "I hung out in the hotel, trying to look like a guest."

"I noticed you," Faye told her. "You looked too young to fit in."

Holden smiled ruefully. "I wish I'd known who you were. I could have saved you some scary moments." She continued her account. "Several times last night and this morning, Draco went back to the meeting site to see if Ms. Evans had showed up. He never found her, but an hour ago he saw Troy hitchhiking south. Draco called me, and I went downhill on foot. Between us we took him into custody."

"He tried to kill Cray," I said. "He planned to kill Faye and me, and—" That brought back my fear of what was to come. "We have to find Barbara, Agent Holden."

She glanced at Draco. "The county guys and the inn staff are already searching, and we'll get more people in to help. And dogs." The tight muscles around her lips told me she believed they'd find a corpse.

After the "We'll leave no stone unturned" speech they always give terrified relatives, Holden went off to speak to her partner. I took hold of Faye's arm. "What if Barbara Ann is—"

Faye cut me off before I said the word. "Margaretta Joy, we're not going to think that way." Faye's taut face told me I was not allowed to even hint Barbara Ann was dead until we were absolutely sure.

Instead of trying to change her mind, I nodded. If Faye wasn't ready to stop hoping, then neither would I. It was harder for me though, because Troy's gloating voice kept drifting through my mind. "…a bad accident."

Holden returned to say that neither Troy nor Gretchen admitted seeing Barbara. "Gretchen says all the 'old broads' looked alike to her, but she was only told to keep track of Mrs. Burner." Holden's head tilted. "I think Troy's hiding something, but it might not apply to Ms. Evans. The man has a lot to hide."

It was time to be completely honest. "I'm pretty sure he…did something to Barbara." I told them about the struggle outside the shed the day before. "He came back later and said—" Tears began again as I finished, though I thought I'd wept them all away in the night. "—he drowned her in the bay."

Faye's arm went around my shoulders, and I heard her speak to Holden as I rested my head on her shoulder and sobbed. "Gretchen said both my sisters were dead, but Retta's right here, alive and well. If she was wrong about Retta, she might be wrong about Barb."

Just then we heard a shout, and I raised my head to look. Deputy Barrett hurried toward us, crossing the road with hardly a glance for oncoming traffic. When he got close enough to speak he said, "One of my men just radioed to say he found a corpse on the beach."

Chapter Forty-five

Barb

Wake up. Wake up!

Light reflected off the placid water and slid through the leaves, making me squint. My mind tried again to regain control, but the rest of me wasn't cooperating. I heard tiny waves lapping. I felt a breeze at my back, humid enough to perhaps signal rain to come. I winced at the scratchy grit on my tongue. And I smelled the damp of decaying leaves. It was an effort, but I involved the fifth of my senses, opening one eye enough to see tree roots before my face with long-dead oak leaves trapped among them.

Something needed me. An image floated along my eyelids—a cat, square-built and self-sufficient. It had a name—a silly name. It needed a better one. Without me, who would scratch its ears and feed it treats? I had a vague idea Dale might, though I wasn't completely sure who Dale was.

Get up. Get up!

I tried. Pulling one arm forward, I pushed myself up out of the sand. The world started spinning, and my stomach threatened to exit through my throat.

There was something I had to do. There was someone I had to meet. There was—it was too much. I sank back to the damp sand.

Chapter Forty-six

Faye

Agent Holden suggested we stay at the inn, but we refused. Promising to stop when she told us to, we followed her out the drive, across the highway, and down the steep decline to the bay. Where the soil turned to beach we turned right, toward a small group of people who stood around a prone form.

Relief flooded my mind as I looked ahead. Even from a distance I could tell the dead person was much larger than Barb and dressed in a water-soaked business suit.

Holden put up a hand and we stopped, as we'd agreed to do. She approached the body, ordering those nearby to back away in their own footprints to preserve the scene as much as possible. I was pretty sure a lot of evidence had been obliterated by searchers and shifting sand, but she did a careful assessment, stopping every few feet to take pictures with her phone and circling the body to get all angles. That the man was dead was obvious from the color of his skin, but she checked his carotid anyway, kneeling carefully and waiting several seconds for a pulse that wasn't there. Beginning with his jacket pocket, she searched the body for identification.

We watched in a combination of fascination and impatience. Finally Retta whispered in my ear, "Why aren't they looking for Barbara?"

"They will," I answered, "but this is going to distract them for a while."

Holden said something to the others before starting toward us. They followed her, and when we were one group she made a general announcement. "It's Roger Engel. I thought I recognized him, and his driver's license confirms it, at least for now. Shot at close range."

I had a moment's thought for Dina. Would she be sorry her father was dead? It might help that he'd apparently come north to deal with Honny's treachery in person, possibly to support her. Roger Engel had misjudged his daughter, believing her incapable of handling a business. That was sad, but he also had badly misjudged Honny. For that, he'd paid with his life.

Retta nudged me, and thoughts of Dina fled. She'd have to deal with her grief. My sister and I had our own family crisis to handle.

Chapter Forty-seven

Retta

The people around us were mostly silent as they waited for the techs who would document the scene. Most seemed stricken, looking for probably the first time in their lives at a murder victim. Others seemed faintly excited, and I imagined them telling friends and family for the next few weeks about the time they were there at the end of a drug lord's career.

No one said anything about the search for Barbara. It would resume soon, but for Faye and me, soon wasn't good enough. "We should go," I murmured, surveying the shore to the south. I pictured what might have happened yesterday. Barbara had started running from Troy at the shed, which was on the south side of the vineyard. If she'd made it to the bay, then what?

"…found it a ways down," an inn employee was telling Agent Holden. "He brought it up to the inn and I put it with the others."

"What was that?" I asked Faye. "What did someone find?"

"A canoe." She pointed. "It was floating down there late yesterday afternoon."

"Come on, then. That's where we need to look." We might have split up and covered more territory, but neither of us suggested it. We needed to be together, whatever we found.

A light rain, the wind, and the waves had swept the sand clear of signs. With nothing to see on the shore we angled into the trees, circling any that had trunks large enough to hide a person.

"You know how they say you'd feel it if someone you love was dead?" Faye asked as we walked. "I don't feel it."

I didn't tell her that was the stuff of fiction. We believe we can sense imminent trouble, but it isn't true. The day my husband was killed had been like any other, and until his brother officers knocked on my door, I had no idea what tragedy had befallen me. If a person can't imagine the world without a loved one, she doesn't.

I turned away from Faye's hopeful expression. Since hearing Troy's cruel account of Barbara Ann's drowning I'd tried to remain optimistic, but in my heart I accepted that she was dead. Faye was still hoping, and I couldn't bear to watch.

That's when I saw a plain, flat sandal sticking out from behind a clump of trees.

Chapter Forty-eight

Barb

I won't bore anyone with a detailed account of what it's like to ride in an ambulance, be admitted to a hospital, and undergo emergency surgery. If you've experienced it you know all about it, and if you haven't, well, good for you.

I don't remember a lot of it anyway. Mostly I recall a vague feeling of relief that someone else was in charge. Faye was there, holding my hand. She kept saying Retta had gone for help that wasn't far away. Then there was a flurry of people around me and the helpless sensation that comes with being strapped down, carried with practiced ease by trained rescuers, and transported by ambulance. People tell you things as you ride along, but only some of them compute. Mostly they talk over you as if you aren't there, and to be honest, you don't really care. Soon there are white ceilings with bright lights, and you move along with swift efficiency, expending no effort whatsoever. Kind people tell you what's going to happen next—not that you care much about that either.

And then there's a long space where you know nothing at all.

I woke several times to find Faye sitting in a chair in a corner. Once she snored softly, resting her chin on her chest. Other times she paged through magazines without much real interest. I thought about saying something to her, but it was too much effort.

Later a doctor came in to talk about gunshot wounds and concussions. Faye was still in the chair, and Retta peered over his shoulder. He asked if I remembered where I was, and I managed to get out a wispy "Yes." He explained what he'd done to repair my shoulder, told me I was lucky the bullet hadn't done more damage than it did, and warned that therapy was in my future. My head trauma was apparently healing nicely.

"I'll see that she does whatever you say," Retta assured him.

I didn't have the energy to argue, but I think I managed to express disapproval with an eyebrow.

Chapter Forty-nine

Faye

Once it was certain Barb would be all right, Retta and I took turns leaving the hospital to provide official statements about what had happened at St. Millicent's. Retta spent a lot of time on the phone with Lars, who wanted to know everything. I spoke to Rory, who blamed himself for some reason.

"Rory, you couldn't have known she'd get shot."

"No." He didn't sound as if he meant it.

"She's going to be fine."

"So you said."

"She doesn't want you to fuss or miss work. She says she'll see you when she gets home."

"That sounds like Barb." He seemed a little less tense. "What does Lars say about all this?"

"Well, Troy eventually told the FBI everything. He got a call from a friend in Detroit warning that Roger was on his way up here. He wanted to take the money and run, but Honny figured it was the perfect time to get rid of Roger and set himself up as the new top man."

"He met Roger on the beach and shot him."

"That's the operating theory." I paused. "All they have to do is track him down."

"They haven't found him yet? It's a peninsula, for Pete's sake."

"His photo is posted everywhere, and he's got no vehicle. It's just a matter of time."

"What about Engel's daughter?"

"She's offered the Bureau full access to his records, which should be a gold mine of associates and conspirators."

I recalled Dina's face when she'd been told her father was dead. Cecily had taken her into her arms like they were old friends, comforting her at first then tending to what needed to be done so Dina didn't have to. I hoped that meant the two women might go forward together, with Dina as designer and Cecily as her assistant. The image made me happy, and I said, "I think she'll be all right."

"And how are you, Faye?"

"I'm sticking close to Barb." In fact I was outside her hospital room, watching her sleep.

"And Retta?"

"She's fine." I sighed. "It was a really scary experience, but we made it through."

Rory chuckled. "Maybe that sister power thing of yours really works. When do you think you'll be back in Allport?"

"If things go well with Barb's shoulder, she'll be released tomorrow. Retta's going back to St. Millicent's with two deputies this afternoon. They'll clear up the details with the inn staff while the Bureau handles the larger concerns, and she's riding along to pick up our things and her car."

"What about Barb's?"

"One of the officers agreed to drive it vehicle back to our hotel in Traverse City. I'll drive her home when she's ready."

"Tell her—" His voice got funny. "Tell her I'll be here."

"Sure thing, Rory."

Chapter Fifty

Retta

Deputies Barrett and Weisnewski couldn't have been nicer, and we chatted about a lot of things on the way to St. Millicent's. Barrett had been reading up on Brad and Angelina, but Weisnewski insisted it was all a publicity thing. I'd long ago lost interest in that particular story, though I buy *People* faithfully and try to keep up on who's with who (Barbara would remind me it should be *whom*, but I think that word is totally archaic and should be dropped from the language).

The weather had turned cool and rainy, but the drive was just as pretty as before. Instead of sunshine, the trees were lit with moisture that made them look deep and impenetrable. And the bay was every bit as impressive in shades of gray as it had been in blue. It was a little creepy riding in the back of a police car though. Talk about feeling closed in!

When we got to the inn, I thanked the deputies for the ride and handed Weisnewski Barbara Ann's car keys. "I'll see you at the Holiday Inn," I told her, and she nodded. As I turned toward my car, I felt a pulse in my jacket pocket. Taking out my phone, I read a message from Rory Neuencamp. *Don't take any chances while that guy is still on the loose.*

Rory's cautious attitude made me smile. He was so much like Barbara Ann, always looking for the shadow in the corner. It was weird though, because the message conjured the image of Troy taking my car keys and sliding them into his pocket. Where had those keys ended up?

"Deputy Barrett, would you wait a minute?"

He was almost to the inn door, but he turned, his handsome face politely interested. "Sure."

"The guy who kidnapped us took my car keys."

"You said you had a spare set in the wheel well."

"Right, but what if he gave them to Honny Bellows?"

"It wouldn't do him any good. We've got roadblocks on the highway." He pointed at my car. "See? It's still here."

I waited, and he finally got it. With a serious glare at the parking lot he said, "He's hiding in there."

"I'm not saying he is, but it's possible. He could come out at night to eat and—whatever. The back windows are tinted, so no one can see in."

"And he can listen to the radio to find out when we pull the roadblocks."

I glanced at my car. "I'm just saying it's possible."

"Wow." Barrett looked very young and decidedly unsure of himself. Was he competent to handle this or should I insist he call for backup? I glanced at Weisnewski, whose hand strayed unconsciously to her sidearm.

"Mrs. Stilson, I need you to go inside and keep everyone there until we come for you."

I opened my mouth to argue, but Barrett said, "Now, ma'am." The friendly manner I'd seen earlier was gone. Weisnewski took a step to the side, forming a line with her partner that sent a silent message. They were the professionals. I should butt out.

Moving past them, I entered the inn. It was almost empty on a Wednesday morning, but I told the desk clerk what was going on and asked her to keep everyone inside. She got on the phone immediately, and I went down the hall to the side door that faced the parking lot. I opened it a slit, eager to know what was happening outside.

Barrett approached my car from the road and Weisnewski from the vineyard side, both with weapons drawn but at their sides. About thirty feet back they stopped, met each other's gaze, planted their feet, and raised their guns. I noted they'd chosen positions that assured they wouldn't be in each other's crossfire if there was shooting.

"Honny Bellows. We know you're in the blue Acadia. Come out with your hands up." Barrett's voice sounded different than before, like the quarterback giving commands on the field sounds so much tougher than that same man doing shaving cream commercials.

Nothing happened.

"Bellows! The next step is tear gas and stun grenades. Come out of there *now*."

Again nothing for a few seconds. Then the back door on the driver's side opened a few inches. "I'm coming out. Don't shoot."

I wanted to warn them not to trust him, but that wasn't necessary. "Unload your gun and drop it onto the ground before you get out."

Seconds later, bullets clattered onto the pavement. Then the gun hit with a metallic clatter.

"Okay." Barrett stepped forward and kicked the gun across to Weisnewski, who picked it up and stowed it in the back of her waistband.

"Come out with both hands in sight," Barrett ordered. "Move slowly and drop to your knees as soon as you're out of the vehicle. Once you're in the position, put your hands on the back of your head, fingers interlaced."

The door opened wider, and a man got out of my car. He wore a hooded sweatshirt over leggings that were a little much for a man his age. I'd never seen him before, but the turquoise flip-flops recalled Faye's description. Stepping away from my car, Honny dropped to his knees, as ordered. When he put his hands behind his head, Weisnewski visibly relaxed.

That was when Honny pulled a second gun from the hood of his shirt and fired at her.

Things happened fast after that. Honny rolled under the car, firing a shot at Barrett as he went. Both officers crouched to make themselves smaller targets and scurried to protected spots. Barrett took cover behind Barbara's Chevy while Weisnewski, apparently unhurt, leapt onto a bench at the vineyard edge, using the back as a shield.

An eerie silence settled on the parking lot.

A voice behind me made me jump. "What's going on out there? Is that the guy they're hunting for?"

I turned to find the desk clerk's face inches from mine. "The police are trying to arrest him," I told her. "So far it isn't going well."

"What should we do?"

"They said to stay inside and let them handle it." Even as I said the words, I was examining the situation. The two officers were pinned down. They'd probably called for assistance, but it would take a while for it to arrive. Looking to where Honny had been a moment before, I didn't see him. He'd rolled out the other side of my vehicle, and I guessed he was standing where one tire or the other hid his feet. It was impossible to tell if he'd come out at the front, where he'd be in position to shoot Barrett, or in the rear, where Weisnewski would be in his sights.

Whichever way he chose, one of the officers was a sitting duck. Once he'd wounded or killed one of them, he could pin the other down while he retreated into the woods and escaped again.

Unless I did something.

On second thought I corrected that. Unless *we* did something.

I turned to the clerk. "What's your name?"

"Bonnie."

"Bonnie, here's what we're going to do. We're each going to take one of those wine casks on the porch and roll it toward the parking lot."

"What?"

I repeated the plan—if you could call it that—adding, "It's a distraction. The deputies can arrest him while he's dodging barrels."

"But he has a gun!"

"He's behind the car, so he can't see us. Take the one on the right."

"And do what again?"

"Turn it on its side and roll it downhill. Try to hit the car, or at least get close." She frowned and I explained, "Any impact should be enough to distract him." She still looked doubtful, so I added, "We have to give the deputies a chance, right?"

After a sigh big enough for a silent movie actress, she nodded.

"Let's go. As soon as you push your barrel, lie flat on the ground and stay there, okay?"

She gulped. "Okay."

We exited the door, taking our respective positions. It was harder than I thought to tip the oaken cask over, and I realized they'd been filled with dirt to keep them in place. I heard Bonnie grunt as she wrestled hers over and got behind it, twisting the barrel a little to aim it where she wanted it to go. That was a vain hope. We had no control over where they ended up, but any distraction was better than none.

When I got my cask on its side I crouched behind it and counted. "One, two, *three!*"

We pushed hard, and the casks started a slow roll down the lawn. Bonnie and I dropped to our stomachs, peeping up to watch where they went. For a few seconds I feared they wouldn't even make it to the parking lot, much less to my car, but the slope was on our side. As the barrels rolled they picked up speed, and when they hit the walkway, there were two loud thumps. They sped up even more.

Of course they didn't go where we'd intended. Adhering to laws of science I never bothered to try to understand, the cask on the right continued more or less on a straight line, but mine took a wide turn, heading almost at right angles to my car. Still, they made a satisfying rumble as they traveled, and soon Honny leaned out to see what was coming at him.

Bonnie's cask was almost upon him. He turned to avoid it, but it caught him a glancing blow on the shoulder as it bounced by and continued downhill. I heard a curse word, and Honny retreated from sight, but the distraction allowed Barrett to move into position behind Barbara's car. When he ordered Honny to drop the second gun, I thought this time it would take.

Beside me Bonnie grinned in elation. "We did it!"

"We did." Her smile turned to a frown. "I hope the boss isn't mad. Those kegs are genuine antiques."

"That's okay," I told her. "Saving lives beats antiques any day. You just became a hero."

Chapter Fifty-one

Barb

"May I come in?" In the doorway of my hospital room stood Angel, the leader of Love-Able Ladies. What was she doing here?

"Please."

She was as carefully dressed, coiffed, and decorated as before, but she seemed less sure of herself. "I wanted to tell you we're all praying for your complete recovery."

Obviously, she'd heard I was a lawyer.

"Nothing that happened at the retreat will be held against you or your organization."

A little line appeared between her brows. "Retta tells me you'll make a full recovery."

I flexed the fingers of my bandaged arm. "No permanent damage; no psychological trauma. As I said, there will be no legal action taken against your group."

She shook her head, as if this wasn't going the way she'd expected. "Ms. Evans, I didn't come here to avoid a lawsuit. I came because you went through a horrible experience. Your sisters were kidnapped. You were shot." She frowned. "That surely wasn't fun."

"Well, no."

"We're very grateful you took on those people and exposed their crimes."

"I suppose we did all right—for a bunch of girls."

Angel licked her lips. "I'm told you are a lifelong advocate for women's rights."

Thanks, Retta. "I disagree with women being encouraged to be content with limited, subservient roles."

"But what if those roles are more important to us than anything we could do somewhere else?" She leaned toward me earnestly. "What if rather than being the first female President, I'd like to raise a son who's the kind of man who's perfect for the job?"

"What if your daughter would make a great President? Do you tell her she can't because she's female?"

Her eyes clouded momentarily. "I would never tell a child of mine she can't do anything she puts her mind to." She smiled almost apologetically. "Women can have influence through the homes we provide and the values we teach."

"So the hand that rocks the cradle rules the world?" I shook my head then remembered that hurt. "I'd rather man up, wear the pants, and get things done."

"But if a woman chooses to rock the cradle instead of trying to rock the world, should she be disparaged for it?"

"Well, no."

"Then we agree. Women can be what they choose. Our little group doesn't hate anyone, and we don't try to convince women to quit their jobs or give up fighting for what they want. Love-Able Ladies just tries to help one kind of woman feel comfortable with being feminine."

"I know you people aren't evil," I admitted. Angel believed in what she was doing, and I believed the opposite. Who was correct? "It's true we talk past each other too often, whether it's women's roles, race, or politics."

She nodded. "If we really listened, we might see we're not so far apart."

"As long as you don't tell little girls they can't be doctors or lawyers."

"Of course they can, but they should also be able to stay home and raise their children without being made to feel like failures."

I thought of the Evans sisters. Though Retta was at heart a Love-Able Lady type, she sat on a half-dozen boards, contributed to the work of several local charities, and served her state and community in a dozen different ways. Faye was neither for feminism nor against it. She'd spent her life being whatever she needed to be, Mom to her own three sons and a host of others as well, despite working full time her whole life and dealing with issues that might have crushed a weaker person. I'd chosen the career-woman path, and while I regretted nothing, I knew my lone-wolf lifestyle wasn't for everyone.

"I understand what you're saying," I told Angel. Swallowing my pride I added, "I had no right to disrupt your event."

"It's good of you to say so." A mischievous glint came into her eye. "But just so you know, I won't be adding your name to the Love-Able Ladies' mailing list."

"No," I replied in a similar tone. "I'm not sure how lovable I am, but I'm quite sure I'll never be known as a sweet, old-fashioned girl."

ABOUT THE AUTHOR

Maggie Pill is also Peg Herring, but Maggie's much younger and cooler.
Visit http://maggiepill.maggiepillmysteries.com and Peg's site http://pegherring.com for more great mysteries.

<u>Have you read Book #1, **The Sleuth Sisters**, yet?</u>
Learn how the sisters started their detective agency, found a long-lost murder suspect, and almost went from three sisters to two.

<u>How about Book #2, *3 Sleuths, 2 Dogs, 1 Murder*</u>?
When Retta's "gentleman friend" is arrested for murder, the sisters brave a winter wilderness, far removed from rescue. Three determined women, with help from two dogs and a pair of horses, can do anything. Sister Power!

<u>Book #3, **Murder in the Boonies**</u>
Renters on the family farm disappear without a trace, and the sisters are left to solve the mystery, deal with a menagerie, and stop a plot that would spell disaster for Michigan's famous Mackinac Island.

Book #4, Sleuthing at Sweet Springs
Visiting a nursing home, Faye meets a woman who claims she doesn't belong there. Trying to help leads the sisters into big trouble, and—who'd have guessed—a flock of helpful chickens!

Books available from Amazon (print, e-book, & audiobook) and Ingram (print only).

Other books by Peg Herring/Maggie Pill

The Simon & Elizabeth Mysteries *(Tudor Era Historical)*
Her Highness' First Murder
Poison, Your Grace
The Lady Flirts with Death
Her Majesty's Mischief
***

The Loser Mysteries *(Contemporary Mystery/Suspense)*
Killing Silence
Killing Memories
Killing Despair
***

Clan Macbeth Historical Romance (medieval Scotland)
Macbeth's Niece
Double Toil & Trouble
***

Standalone Mysteries
Somebody Doesn't Like Sarah Leigh (contemporary cozy mystery)
Her Ex-GI P.I. ('60s-era mystery)
A Lethal Time and Place ('60s-era paranormal mystery)
Shakespeare's Blood (thriller)

Thriller with Cozy Tendencies
KIDNAP.org